PASSING THE BUCK!

"Mr. Bucher, three bandits of Arab nationality, each armed with a powerful rifle, have
barricaded themselves on the roof of the
Secretariat Building at the United Nations
in a battle-to-the-death protest of Israel's being willed plans for the hydrogen motor by
Shazar. They demand that a copy of the plans
be delivered to them by the U.S. Secretary of
State—which the President will never agree
to—"

"How high is the U.N.'s Secretariat Building?"

"Five hundred and fifty feet—thirty-nine
stories; and we can't clear the area and starve
them out if that's what you're thinking. They
have one of the building's security guards.
They swear they'll throw him off the top if
their demands are not met by sundown."

Bucher stared at the phone in his hand.
"Jesus James H. Christ," he at last intoned
absently. Then: "So what do you plan on
doing?"

"I've just done it," the director said. "I've
just passed the buck to you. It's your baby
now, Bucher . . ."

The Butcher Series:

The Butcher
The U. N. Affair
by Stuart Jason

PINNACLE BOOKS • NEW YORK CITY

The Butcher: The U.N. Affair

Copyright © 1976 by Script Representatives, Inc.

An original Pinnacle Books edition, published for the first time anywhere.

ISBN: 0-523-00843-0

First printing, April 1976
Second printing, September 1976

Cover Art by Fred Love

Printed in the United States of America

PINNACLE BOOKS, INC.
275 Madison Avenue
New York, N.Y. 10016

THE U.N. AFFAIR

1

Bucher sat with his back to a corner of the sleazy West Side bar that was registered at City Hall, License Division, as Bozeman's Bar; it belonged to Bozeman Curdi but was known throughout the neighborhood as Curdi's Crudhouse. This latter appelation, Bucher was forced to acknowledge to himself, seemed by far the more appropriate, due to the sour, dank smell hovering inside the place, the cheap and shabby furnishings, and the overall aura of filth in the making, all of which was made worse by the man behind the bar, Bozeman Curdi himself—or what was left of Bozeman Curdi—though no one ever called him Bozeman after meeting him the first time. After that, it wasn't Boze, it was "Hey you" or "Hey boy." Even so, Bucher felt a tinge of pity for the man, for he and Boze Curdi had one thing in common. They both had once been Syndicate personnel, but now they were not. Bucher was still alive because he was quick with a gun and had the survival instincts of a jungle-bred predator; Bozeman, simply because, in the Syndicate's eyes, he wasn't worth killing. That is, Bozeman did not know enough about the Syndicate's operations to make him dangerous. The man had only been at the first rung of the Syndicate's success ladder when he met and married singer-dancer Lorili Popjoy Lamour, a scheming, avaricious, hard-as-nails wench whose tactics for getting ahead in New York made even certain hardened Syndicate cutthroats frown in distaste.

Shortly after their marriage Boze Curdi began hitting the bottle, and the rumor spread that he had caught his one and only belly-rubbing with one of the Syndicate hierarchy. Whether it was true or false, and Bucher had never heard anything to make him disbelieve the rumor, Curdi had hugged the bottle all the way down to skid row and through the divorce his wife obtained within a year of their wedding day.

Bucher glanced up at the clock behind the bar before he spoke; it was nine-thirty in the evening and White Hat's director was due to show any minute. "Is this your normal evening rush hour, Boze?"

Boze Curdi sidled toward Bucher from where he had been slouched against the back bar some ten feet away, the hang-dog air of defeat about the man so real it was almost tangible.

"Ain't nobody never comes in here much, Butchy," he said in the servile tone of an acknowledged inferior. "Maybe some of the boys I used to know on skid row comes in once in a while to mooch a few drinks, but that's all. Ain't nobody never comes in here much." He stopped at a sink filled with dirty glasses and ashtrays and commenced washing them vigorously, the clink of glass filling the long bar with unnecessary noise. Through the low-level din Bucher thought once he heard the dialing of a phone and looked quickly toward the booth to one side of him, but the booth was empty. Then the phone behind the bar, some twenty feet beyond the cash register, pealed shrilly. Boze Curdi hurried to answer it, doing so in a thick, unintelligible mumble Bucher made no attempt to overhear. Curdi was still on the phone a minute or so later when Sam White, White Hat's small, stooped director, entered. Without a word he took a stool beside Bucher at the bar, then:

"Two of our boys are covering the alley entrance in back and two the front. You been here long?"

"About ten minutes," Bucher told him. "It takes almost as long to reach here from the airport as it does to fly from Miami to New York. What's the big deal? It sounded urgent." Before the director answered, he continued: "I suppose you know I was on my way to Puerto Rico?"

3

"I'm sorry," White said doggedly. "Yes. I know. And as quick as this Jewish-Arab hassle at the United Nations is smoothed over, you can return to Puerto Rico. How is Kleyr, by the way? I understand you called her in Arecibo from Cuba."

"She's all right, as far as I know," Bucher chuckled, recalling the vivacious, explosive spitfire Kleyr Boriquen. "At least she was when I left Arecibo a week ago for Cuba."

The director looked away, his expression something like that of the cat that ate the goldfish, clearly not wanting to answer Bucher on the subject. Again Bucher said:

"It sounded urgent. What's the deal?"

"A couple of weeks ago *Time* magazine picked up a story from the *Boston Globe* that claimed, on pretty damn good authority, that Israel has a secret arsenal of ten atomic weapons. Israel of course denied it and, because they had little choice in the matter, the Arabs—"

"You're speaking of the Jews and the Arabs here in the United States?" Bucher cut in.

"I'm speaking of the Jews and the Arabs right here in New York," Sam White declared emphatically. "Both the American Jews and Arabs and those in the United Nations."

"Israel denied the secret arsenal of ten atomic weapons and the Arabs had little choice in the matter—so what happened?"

"Have you ever heard of Nabil Chehade Shazar?"

"The famous American inventor? Christ, who

hasn't heard of him? But I thought he was dead."

"Shazar was also a Jew—and he is dead. Two months now. His will was registered in probate court day before yesterday, the same day you were winding up the Cubano caper. And in his will Shazar left, in joint ownership between the United States and Israel, detailed plans for the manufacture of an inexpensive, virtually maintenance-free hydrogen-powered motor—"

"That would give the States and Israel access to the world's greatest energy source," Bucher cut in again.

"Right," Sam White agreed. "Hydrogen."

Bucher chuckled in spite of the other's doleful expression. "And leave the Arabs squatting on their oil cans in the Middle East with no one to embargo but each other."

"Right again."

"I thought you were pro-Jewish. White Hat scuttlebutt claims you scored twenty-seven Nazis in World War II. With a knife in hand-to-hand."

Sam White's face became reflective. "Yeah. We never counted the ones we killed with a gun or grenade. That was against the rules—and it was also over thirty years ago and doesn't solve our problem now."

"Just exactly what the hell is our problem?" Bucher asked tersely. "I'd like to get back to Kleyr and Puerto Rico."

"Our problem is to prevent an open outbreak of hostilities betwen American Jews and Arabs and to protect the Israeli and Arab bloc nations' missions to the United Nations. Specifically, to prevent an outbreak between the JDL, the Jewish Defense League, and the Al Fat'ha. I don't think we'll have too much trouble protecting the UN missions. It's the locals that have me bugged. You ever heard of a joker by the name of Ahmed Fowzie?"

"American?"

"American, yes, of naturalized Arab parents—so he claims."

"What's his background?"

"We can't learn a damn thing about him," Sam White said in disgust. "None of the usual sources are any help; he doesn't even have a Social Security number."

"So what's Fowzie's pitich?" Bucher asked, puzzled.

"Well—he's a damn good salesman for one thing. He's got the local Arabs, and especially the powerful Al Fat'ha, believing that he can solve their problems with the Jews."

"That sounds familiar as hell," Bucher snorted. "What's on the son of a bitch's mind? To solve the Jewish problem a la Hitiler? I can solve our problem right quick—"

"White Hat's?" This time it was the director who interrupted.

"Why not? I'll burn the son of a bitch. That'll take care of Ahmed Fowzie. Where does the bastard hang out?"

"Hey! Slow down!" The director grabbed his arm as Bucher started to rise from the bar stool.

"I've had my suspicions, though you never said."
The director chuckled heartily, even happily. "I
didn't know you were violently pro-Jewish."

"Yeah," Bucher replied in a voice that could
mean anything. After a moment he relaxed and
resumed his seat, his face looking less like flesh-
colored granite. The director shook his gray head
in wonder.

"I thought I had it bad, but— For how long?"

"Since I quit the Syndicate," Bucher growled.
"Before then I couldn't think of any human being
but myself, but since I quit it's different. And I
don't know why. That's just the way it is. Preju-
dice, bigotry, and organized, aggressize ignorance
all make my blood boil."

"And there's Kleyr also," the director chuckled
again. "I understand she expects you to father
her twelve *oyfele*—I don't know the plural for
baby in Yiddish."

Surprised etched Bucher's hard features. "Who
told you Kleyr was Jewish?"

"I—well—uh—" White Hat's director looked
extremely uncomfortable all of a sudden. "Why—
her name, of course. Kleyr." He refused to meet
Bucher's eye. Then there wasn't time.

The front door of Bozeman's Bar exploded inward with sounds only slightly less deafening
than a thunderous crash and the neat, petite, and
thoroughly captivating subject of their conversation rushed toward Bucher, arms outstretched.

"Oh, Boo, darling!" she wailed plaintively. "It's
been over a week since you left Arecibo for Cuba

and—" Barely within reach of Bucher she stopped, swung.

Crack! Her small fist bounced off his hard jaw like an eight ball off the side rail. He grabbed it with his left hand.

"What the hell's going on here!" But his stern expression served for naught before Kleyr's vivacious and breathtaking Latin beauty. Especially when she sprang forward, this time both arms circling his neck, soft lips hunting his. Sam White cleared his throat noisily half a dozen times and in intense yet restrained delight.

"I'll wait at the other end of the bar," he at last declared in a loud voice. He would have liked to leave the bar then and there, but Bucher had to know sooner or later, so . . .

"Hey, man," a deep basso profundo said from the far end of the room, at the rear entrance. "You that ol' bad-ass butcher boy?"

"Huh-h!" the director said quietly. "Already we got problems."

Instinctively Bucher turned, shoving Kleyr behind him.

"That's me," Bucher told the red-haired giant who was literally filling the rear door. The blade of the shiv in the man's hand was at least nine inches long, thick and heavy, and the man held it by the blade, a sure sign he knew how to throw it.

"Take care of Kleyr," Bucher said to the director without removing his eyes from the red-haired intruder. Then to Red Hair, wanting to get the hassle behind him, he said: "What's on your

8

BB-sized brain, you fruity looking sonofabitch?"

"Who you callin' fruity?" the man snarled. "I'm here to pin you to the wall—!" The arm with the long knife whipped up and back and an evil grin of triumph spread over his flushed face as—

"Koosh! Koosh!"

The ugly, thick-barreled, silencered Walther P–38 that appeared as if by magic in Bucher's big mitt sighed twice, gently, but second sigh was smothered by Red Hair's agonized scream. The first 9mm slug from the Walther clipped the four fingers off his knife hand; the second smashed the knife itself back out through the open rear door. The man wheeled and fled, screams drifting back like streaks of smoke from a rushing loco-motive.

"What was that all about?" Kleyr asked calmly; she had long since adjusted herself to the un-expected, explosive, ofttimes grisly violence that occurred in her man's life.

"I'm not sure," Bucher said thoughtfully, leathering his piece. "But one thing I can be sure of: somebody spotted me at the airport when my plane landed from Miami—so the word's out."

"What I'd like to know is what happened to my two men guarding the rear entrance of this joint," the director declared angrily, heading for the back door. He never made it.

"You ain't goin' nowhere, bub." The black man who suddenly appeared in the empty rear door was as large, if not larger, than Red Hair. Nor was the apelike white character following in his

9

footsteps much smaller. The hands of both men were empty, which told Bucher they intended to use only their hands as weapons. A quick, joyous thrill of exultation shot through his big frame.

"You must be the Butcher," the black man said to Bucher, flexing his massive hands and rolling his shoulders to loosen their bulging muscles.

"That's right." Bucher strode easily toward the glowering pair, hands in coat pockets. "And this is my night to take people apart for the fun of it. Who's first?"

The black man shook his head briefly in admiration. "They said you had guts. I'll have to give them credit for not lying."

"Give who credit?" Bucher asked casually, still walking easily toward them.

"Ahmed Fowzie, man. Who else? He says to squash you and we're here to squash you."

"Can that ape with you talk?" Bucher asked, indicating the second man with a nod. "How come you don't have him on leash?"

A dull, threatening rumble came from Ape's barrel chest and his top lip snarled upward to reveal fanged molars. But he did not say a word.

"You want to send Ape back to Ahmed 'Yellow Belly' Fowzie with word that I clobbered you?" Bucher continued to walk toward the black man, stopping an arm's length away.

"You ain't clobbered me yet, man," the man chuckled gloatingly—and swiftly reached for Bucher.

Bucher's hands came out of the coat pockets

armored with murderous brass knucks. He clubbed the massive black hands aside easily, almost indifferently, and struck, the black man's eyes bulging dangerously in pain and surprise when the knucks on Bucher's right hand shelled his teeth like corn. Then Bucher's left whipped up with startling speed, caught the man under the chin, and he heard the gratifying, whispery crunch as the jawbone crumpled. Then sagged. The man seized his face, became fully aware of the damage an instant before pain struck, and released a chilling, gurgly howl, then leaped high into the air, first on one foot and then on the other. At a quick move from the other man, Bucher whipped out the Walther—

"Crack!"

—in time to see the tiny .22 caliber hole appear in his low forehead. The man sighed gustily between two guttural howls from the black man, dropped the .45 he had yanked from a rear pocket, and crumpled to the floor without another sound.

It was not necessary for Bucher to turn to see that Kleyr had shot the Ape with her little French-made Unique D.E.S. 69, the finest small-bore match target pistol in the world. In Puerto Rico Bucher had seen her hit a twenty-five-cent piece nine times out of ten at fifty meters. What puzzled him was why the hell she had the pistol with her in the first place. And why the hell was she here in New York instead of in Arecibo, Puerto Rico, where she belonged?

Instead of turning to Kleyr and the director,

11

Bucher made as if to clout the howling black man with his mailed fist again, and the man duplicated the action of Red Hair. He fled. Without so much as a casual glance at the dead man, Bucher then turned, his cold eyes noting the terrified figure of Boze Curdi behind the bar. The man trembled like an aspen in the wind, his face the ashen hue of death.

"Tell the cops I killed the bastard when he tried to rob you, Boze." Then Bucher walked over to Kleyr and studied her lovely face a long moment in silence.

"Now what the hell's this all about, Princess?" he said at last. "You in New York, and with a gun. Why?"

2

Kleyr gave a fetching pout, caught it, and demanded bluntly: "Why did you not return to Puerto Rico from Cuba instead of going to Miami?"

Bucher indicated the director. "Business. I phoned—"

"Business?" she spat in acid tones which did not quite ring true. What's more, both she and Bucher knew it did not ring true. A second later she was again in his arms, weeping profusely, overjoyed at being with her Boo again.

Bucher held her without speaking, memory sweeping him eight years into the past when they'd first met, when he had known her as simply another student at Cornell University, not as the incredible genius who, before her fourteenth birthday, had offered to the scientific world a thin, compact volume titled K. M. Boriquen's *Syllurgics*, a study dealing analytically with fourth-dimension mathematics. The scientific world had been joy-stunned by the book, he learned later, and simply stunned, period, on learning its author was hardly fourteen years old, just as Bucher had been stunned, and filled with self-revulsion when, near the end of the first week they had been delight-fully ensconced at Hibbings Lodge in the Cat-skills, he also had discovered quite by accident that Kleyr was only a few weeks past fourteen. He had left her without a word, sick in his very soul—and Kleyr had attempted suicide. Eight years had passed. Then, less than two months ago, he had been on a mission to Puerto Rico, and again they had met—with Kleyr declaring, and he agreeing, that there would be no more separa-tions. Before the mission was completed she was naming the twelve children she planned for them to have. They had been enjoying life to the fullest on a secluded, non-touristy Puerto Rican beach when an urgent plea from White Hat interrupted, sending Bucher to Cuba with instructions to squelch an assassination attempt on Fidel Castro. This had been only last week. Bucher had stopped off at Miami on his way back to Kleyr and Puerto Rico when another urgent message had asked him to fly to New York instead. And now he was in New York. But so was Kleyr. He wanted to know why. He looked questioningly over the top of Kleyr's glossy curls at White Hat's director. Sam

White shrugged expressively and made a gesture implying that Kleyr wanted to tell Bucher herself.

"Anyway," the director said hurriedly, "I've got to see what happened to my two men out back."

"Here." Bucher released Kleyr and gave her his handkerchief. "Blow."

She funny-faced him impishly and whispered: "In public?"

Bucher knew he would get nothing serious from her at present. Later—

"Yes, later," Kleyr said, evincing her peculiar talent of reading his thoughts. "And later, lout, I'll have you bushed to such a frazzle you won't care why I'm in New York. You'll just be glad I'm here. You'll also be too weak to do anything about it." She biffed his chin affectionately with a small fist. "So there. Now let's get to my hotel and I'll teach you about the birds and bees." Without seeming to have noticed the man before, she whirled to where Boze Curdi stood across the bar. "Don't gape, stupid! He's my husband and I'll teach him whatever I choose." She tugged Bucher's arm. "Come on, lout. Come with Momma."

"How the hell did you get past the two guards at the front door?" Bucher demanded suddenly.

"I seduced them, dammit! Both of them! Standing up! Now come on!"

Bucher fixed Boze Curdi with cold eyes. "Where can I find Ahmed Fowzie?"

"Ah-Ah-Ahmed F-F-Fowzie?" the sickly white Curdi bleated in terror. "He ain't n-n-never b-been in h-here. Honest to G-God he ain't."

"I asked where could I find him, dammit!"

"I ain't never h-heard of n-no Ahme-duh F-Fowzie."

Bucher motioned toward the rear door. "You know any of the three goons who bid for me tonight?"

Curdi shook his head so violently his teeth clicked.

"Boo," Kleyr said quietly from beside Bucher. "The poor man is terrified of you, of what's taken place here tonight. If you must question him, cannot you do it later? When he has his wits about him?"

Instead of answering, Bucher watched Sam White herd two sheepish-looking White Hat agents through the back door.

"Things have come to a sorry pass when one lone man casually walks up and cold-cocks two of my men like that red-haired goon whose fingers you shot off did," the director said grimly to Bucher as he and the two younger men walked past. "I'll phone you tomorrow at Kleyr's hotel."

"Right," Bucher replied, knowing the director was mistaken; he and Kleyr were not going to Kleyr's hotel. "Where are you staying?" he asked her as the director and his men disappeared into the night outside.

"The New York Hilton."

"Good. Then we go to the New York Hilton." But they didn't. They took a taxi in a long, roundabout route to where Bucher had earlier parked his rented Olds sedan, several blocks from Bozeman's Bar. They stopped once, while he made a brief telephone call, then proceeded, by another long, roundabout route, to a ten-story parking lot, parked on the top floor, and walked across several roofs before going through the skylight on one of them.

"Boo," Kleyr whispered in honest perplexity. "Where are we?"

Bucher did not answer until they had passed down a short hallway and he had unlocked a door with a key he took from his pocket.

"We're in the Carlton Hotel," he told her quietly, following her into the lavish high-fashion apartment done in white panels with gilt edges.

"Oooh!" Kleyr gasped excitedly at the sight of it. "It's French. I love French decor. Look—it reminds me of pictures I've seen of Marie Antoinette's boudoir."

"Pictures?" Bucher smiled, happy because she was happy.

"Oh, paintings, silly, I—" She froze in place as she watched him close and lock a second door over the first, this second one made of inch-thick steel plate. "Boo, what are you doing?" Her tone held an oddly strained note.

"This is New York, Princess," he told her calmly. "And there's still a quarter of a million dollars dead-only reward on my head."

"That—steel door?"

He nodded. "I rent this place year round. Neither the hotel's management nor any of the help have ever seen me; I rented it by phone several years ago. The management thinks I'm a diamond courier. That's the reason I gave for having the suite lined with steel plate and re-furnished as it was before."

"Does Sam—and White Hat—know about this place?"

Now it was Bucher who froze in place, his tone that held the oddly strained note. "Kleyr, for God's sake, what do you know about White Hat? Who told you?"

She looked at him archly, suppressing a grin of excitement. "When the frost is on the pumpkin there's joy in the icebox."

Instinctively Bucher felt behind him for the chair and dropped into it heavily, never taking his eyes off the petite, dainty woman before him; the idiotic expression she had just voiced was White Hat's ID code number twenty-three—something she could never know without being a member of the organization.

"Who permitted you to join White Hat?" he whispered hoarsely, knowing there was only one person who could do such a thing. *"God damn Sam White!"* he roared suddenly, for once letting his temper overcome his better judgment. *"I'll kill that son of a bitch!"* He leapt from the chair, hard face white with rage—

"Boo!" Kleyr caught him around the neck. "Boo! Listen to me! Sam couldn't help himself! Anyway, I learned about White Hat from you!" He pushed her away.

18

"What?" About to unlock the steel panel door and go for a settlement with White Hat's director, Bucher whirled. *"I* told you?"

"No, dear," Kleyr said, clinging to him again. "You didn't *tell* me. I didn't say that. I said I learned it from you."

"How?" Bucher said, speaking almost civilly again. "How from me if I didn't tell you? I don't talk in my sleep."

"I know, dear. But I read lips. Now make with your characteristic 'I be goddamn,' dear."

"I be goddamn," Bucher intoned slowly in surprise, hearing nothing she had said after "I read lips." "I be goddamn." Then: "But White let you join, the bastard!"

"No, Boo. You're mistaken, dear. I blackmailed Sam White into letting me join White Hat."

"You blackmailed Sam White?"

"Mmm-huh," Kleyr replied coquettishly, pushing Bucher back and down into the overstuffed chair once again, then plopping down on his lap. "I told him if he didn't let me join and be with you then I'd send you a message that unless you joined me in Puerto Rico at once that this time I would be successful at what I failed at that time you deserted me at Hibbings Lodge in the Catskills."

"Jesus," Bucher said quickly. "Don't talk like that. You frighten hell out of me when you talk suicide."

"Oh, silly! I was only bluffing." She nuzzled

19

his neck. "But Sam White didn't know that." She was silent for a moment. "Boo?"

"Yeah?"

"Let's shower and go to bed, huh? I'm pooped."

"So you actually bluffed him into letting you join the organization, eh?" Bucher grinned, imagining the sweaty time she must have given White Hat's small director, his anger at the man dissolving.

"You didn't hear a word I said," Kleyr pouted, leaving his lap and commencing to undress. "All you can think about is business-business-business."

"Kleyr," Bucher said solemnly, repeatedly pointing with a forefinger toward a window, indicating the world outside. "This is New York, Princess, and the streets out there are filled with sharks just waiting to gobble up a tender little minnow like you."

"Gobble me up like that apish character in the bar did tonight?"

Bucher opened his mouth to speak; he'd forgotten the speed and skill with which she'd dispatched the man. Then he closed it again with a click. What the hell was the use? She could out-think him in half a minute, or less, so talking simply did no good. Unless—

"Boo-Boo, come on," she insisted impatiently, looking around inquisitively.

"In there." Bucher pointed toward a door. "That's the bedroom. The shower is beyond." Unless he had some leverage—which he had powerful evidence to suspect he just might have, by God! It was sort of a dirty trick, but he simply could not have her tagging around with him here in New York. The Syndicate would at once latch onto her as a way of getting at him; then— An icy chill trickled up and down Bucher's spine. He refused to think of what might happen to her then.

"Boo!" Kleyr wailed from the doorway of the bedroom. "Are you coming or not?"

"I'm not," Bucher said curtly.

"Wh-what?"

"What about the twelve children you've got planned? No wife of mine makes a target of herself for hopped-up Syndicate gunsels. You resign from White Hat now, immediately, or we've had it."

A thick, weighty silence ensued until she said: "Do you mean that, Boo?"

"I mean every damn word of it," he declared firmly—and by the time he had finished declaring it, she had prissed across the room in all her ravishing, mind-numbing nudity to where he now stood and, raising on tiptoes, pecked his chin affectionately with her lips.

"Very well, Boo," she said contritely. "Since there can be only one head of any household, then you'll be the head of our household." To herself she added silently: "And I'll be the neck that turns the stubborn head. When necessary."

Taken completely by surprise at her unexpected submission to his demand, Bucher was for the moment caught without words, his attempt to speak producing nothing but an inarticulate sound.

"Oooh, goody!" Kleyr clapped her hands and bounced with a great show of joy. "Already his tongue's so stiff he can't talk." Whereupon she fled squealing through the bedroom into the bath, where Bucher joined her under the shower a couple of minutes later.

"Shall I apologize and say I was teasing?" she asked while washing his back.

"Were you teasing?" Bucher grinned over his shoulder.

"I was not. Remember that time—those dozens of times at Hibbings Lodge, and I kept passing out?"

"And the pillow you ripped apart at Arecibo?"

"And that tiny atoll east of Puerto Rico where we flew to that night in the big Chinook helicopter when you thought someone was trying to kill me? What was the name of that atoll?"

"Barefoot."

"Yes. Barefoot. I got tipsy on champagne and held a conversation with the man in the moon?" Suddenly the sparkle left her voice; she sobered immediately. "Oh, Boo, I'll be so glad when all this silliness between Jew and Arab is over and we can return home to Arecibo."

Dawn was tinting the eastern sky the following morning when Bucher awoke to the fragrance of freshly brewed coffee and other mouth-watering smells coming from the direction of the suite's kitichen. He was drawing on pajama bottoms when Kleyr's lovely face, cheeks tinged faintly pink in her happiness, peeked around the edge of the doorway.

"All right, gunfighter, up an' at 'em. Time to pod your sides and sally forth to feats of derring-do."

Bucher laughed, feeling good. "Where'd you get the expression 'pod your sides'?"

"I read a book once; it's East Tennessee colloquial."

"Can I eat without a top to these pajamas?"

"Of course not. But I'll wear it. See?" She stepped into full view, entrancing in the outlandishly oversize top to his pajamas. And nothing else. The sleeves of the garment were rolled up to the shoulders, but the shoulders themselves hung down to her elbows. "Okay?"

"Okay." Bucher grinned so hard his face hurt.

They ate in the dining room, she on his lap, at times feeding him from her plate.

"All that food in the pantry, Boo," she said at last. "That pantry is full, stuffed, and so is the freezer. How big is that freezer?"

"Twenty-seven cubic feet." Bucher poured them both another cup of coffee.

"But why, Boo? All that food, that big medicine cabinet in the bathroom, steel plate under the wall paper. This is a fort instead of an apartment."

"That's exactly what it's meant to be," Bucher

23

told her. "A fort. And this is where you stay until I finish this hassle between the Jews and the Arabs, understand?"

"Yes, Boo." She glanced at her watch. "What say we finish our coffee in the big room, huh? It's time for an early morning TV newscast."

Kleyr's watch was a bit slow, for when the picture tube warned, it revealed that the weather foreeast was already in progress. Bucher listened with only half an ear, his mind busy on the problems confronting him. His first task, of course, was to try to locate Ahmed Fowzie; the crud must have a big, smooth-running organization to have spotted him at the airport last night, then sent three goons to Bozeman's Bar to chill him. That took a real smooth-running organization. The weatherman wound up his forecast as Bucher finished his coffee and set the cup on a table at the end of the sofa—and froze in place when the camera switched back to the newscaster, who said:

"And in conclusion, ladies and gentlemen, once again the names of the five members of Israel's mission to the United Nations who have disappeared. The three men: Jacob Radak, Abel Yaakovi, Haim ben Brozai; and the two women: Mili Mandelbaum and Ruth Reichman. All five are members of Israel's permanent mission to the United Nations and, according to police, were dragged from their vehicle by masked bandits within a few blocks of 800 Second Avenue, the Israeli Consulate General's office in New York, and forced into another vehicle, which at the moment is the object of an intensive statewide search. Keep tuned . . ."

"Boo!" Kleyr dashed into the bedroom after Bucher. Already he was jerking on his clothes.

"What's the name of that Arab outfit here in New York?" he growled. "Al-something-or-other."

"Al Fat'ha?"

"Yeah. Al Fat'ha. Know anything about the organization?"

"Only what Sam told me yesterday. It's headed by a man called the Wog. His real name is Ali Annaser."

"American?"

"New York."

"And the Jewish Defense League—who heads it?"

"For the past few weeks Rabbi Levi Shimesh. The JDL's leadership changed recently. Shimesh is American also."

Bucher nodded, buttoning his shirt. "I'll call White Hat on where to locate this Wog bastard and the Rabbi."

"Wait a sec." Kleyr left the bedroom and Bucher could hear her at the writing table beyond the TV; she was gone less than a minute. "Here." She gave him a piece of Carlyle stationery with Rabbi Shimesh's name and address and that of the Wog, Ali Annaser.

"Annaser's hangout is 99 Names? A theater?" Bucher frowned. "In the Village?"

"Uh-huh. One of the Off-Broadway things. It

belongs to Annaser. The productions are always in Arabic and more or less typical of life in the Middle Eastern Arabian world. I understand they're always filled with anti-Semitic propaganda.... Boo?"

"Yeah?"

"What are you going to do?"

"First see Rabbi Shimesh, then the Wog."

"And?"

"Hell, play it by ear, Princess. If I knew exactly what I was going to do I'd have this particular rat race already closed and we'd be headed for Puerto Rico." He jabbed a forefinger in her direction. "You stay here, understand?"

"Yes, dear," Kleyr replied meekly—a bit too meekly, though Bucher did not notice.

"And if I call, we speak in Che-Che, huh?" Che-Che was their own private language which they had constructed. Or rather, Kleyr had constructed most of it, while Bucher had been forced to strain his mental powers to the utmost simply to keep up with her.

Che-Che was simplicity itself, much simpler than Esperanto, with a few exceptions, and it had been these exceptions that had all but clobbered Bucher. One was verb suffixes. In conjugating the Spanish verb "to speak" one finds exactly one hundred and three forms; in Che-Che there were exactly ten thousand seven hundred and twelve for the same word, a different suffix for each different day of a fortnight. Kleyr had arranged them in a simple code form which made it unnecessary for Bucher to memorize them all or he'd never have been able to master the language. And there were other exceptions, such as pronouns being direct objects one day, reflexive the next, indirect objects another, and so on. Then, of course, there was the key phrase that had to be used at the onset of any conversation between them, the key designating which day, or which number between one and fourteen, was to be used, or one would not know what the other was talking about.

"Yes, dear," Kleyr said again. "If you call me here we'll speak in Che-Che."

North of Manhattan's financial district, and over to the east, is an area known to New Yorkers as the Lower East Side. This is traditionally the immigrants' section of New York and, Bucher noted with satisfaction, despite the incursion of housing projects and modern buildings, it was still a colorful, bustling area of markets, shops, tenements, and tiny factories. It was also the neighborhood of the Jewish ghetto. It was here that Bucher found Rabbi Shimesh, in a small, two-story dwelling back off the street at the far end of a fenced yard that reminded Bucher of a postage stamp. Twice he checked the address Kleyr had given him, for the building had certain earmarks of being deserted, among them the fact that the windows of the second story were covered by thick boards. Yet the address matched, so Bucher parked the rented maroon Olds sedan at the nearest space—two blocks away—and walked back.

On the tiny front porch of the building Bucher saw numerous scars that remarkedly resembled scars made by shrapnel; they *were* scars made by shrapnel, for in several places the jagged fragments yet remained. Moreover, now that he was close, he saw that the downstairs windows were boarded up on the *inside*—and there was a tiny peephole in the thick, heavy oak door that had the head of a large bolt showing in each corner.

"I be goddamn," Bucher muttered, willing to gamble that the bolt held a sheet of steel to the inside surface of the door.

He heard no sound from inside the house in response to his ringing the doorbell, yet suddenly, instinctively, he knew he was being observed through the peephole in the door. The instinct proved accurate a moment later when a masculine voice, deep and vibrant, yet carrying that peculiar, reedy sound a small electronic speaker would give it, said from directly over his head:

"Yes? Who is it?"

"Rabbi Shimesh?" Bucher glanced upward quickly as he spoke, saw the small four-inch speaker in the porch ceiling near a light bulb. "Rabbi Shimesh, my name is Bucher and I must speak with you concerning the five members of Israel's mission to the United Nations who were kidnapped."

"I have nothing to say to the police," the speaker above Bucher's head said.

28

Bucher squeezed his eyes tightly together, cudgeling his brain for the precise words of the ancient Hebrew language Kleyr had taught him. At last they fell into place and, swiftly, to be certain, he ran them through his mind before giving them utterance, then said: "Rabbi Shimesh, please believe me. I am a friend and I was given your name and address by a friend of yours." He hoped this last was correct. Kleyr had not said she knew the rabbi personally. There was a long silence before any sound came again from beyond the door; then the man's voice, in the same ancient Semitic tongue, asked:

"And the name of my friend who sent you?"

"Kleyr Boriquen."

Almost instantly from beyond the door came the muted rattle of heavy chains, then the removing of a bar from across it. A second later the door was pulled wide and Bucher thought to himself: "My god! He's even bigger than that goon who tried to shiv me at Bozeman's Bar last night."

"Come in, Mr. Bucher. Come in." The bearded, middle-aged giant motioned him inside with a hand the size of a baseball glove. "I'm Rabbi Shimesh." The voice now, coming directly from the man and not over the tiny speaker, sounded not only deep and vibrant but almost as if it were coming from a cavern due to the Rabbi's enormous barrel chest. Bucher winced involuntarily when they shook hands. Rabbi Shimesh immediately barred and chained the door—and Bucher noted that he had been correct in assuming the door was armored. It looked a lot like the front door of his suite at the Carlyle.

"And how is my little Puerto Rican genius?" the rabbi boomed fondly, his sharp, intelligent eyes studying Bucher's face with meticulous care.

"Fine," Bucher told him. "Just fine—and I apologize for disturbing you at this early hour, but the situation demands it."

The old man nodded understandingly. "Come. Let us go upstairs to my study. I do not live downstairs." He waved a hand, indicating the room in general. "You see how the door is armored; the entire house is the same under the finish, and it is more difficult to get a bomb upstairs. So I live upstairs. Come."

Bucher did not have to be told that Rabbi Shimesh lived alone. Virtually everything he saw indicated it, but especially the huge study, the walls of which offered the added protection of books that covered them from floor to ceiling. The desk, an enormity of four by ten feet of black mahogany, somehow became dwarfed when Rabbi Shimesh sat down behind it, motioning Bucher to a deep leather chair to one side.

"Now Mr. Bucher," he rumbled. "What is it that I can do for you?"

Bucher laid it on the line. "You can keep the Jewish Defense League from attacking Al Fat'ha until I have a try at locating the five kidnapped Israelis." A dozen slow heartbeats passed, Rabbi Shimesh's shrewd, intelligent eyes locked with his, one huge forefinger thumping the desk top in measured rhythm, until the older man said quietly:

"Really, Mr. Bucher? And how do you propose to find them?"

"By finding Ahmed Fowzie."

Another long silence, then: "I see. And when you find Ahmed Fowzie what will you do? Ask him to release the five?"

"I'll kill the son of a bitch."

3

An ordinary person might have been shocked at Bucher's forthright reply, or frightened, or revolted, but Rabbi Shimesh was no ordinary person, so he threw his great head back and rocked in his chair, his thunderous laughter shaking the rafters. At this early hour he wore only shirt and trousers, and as he laughed he stretched his arms out to the side and Bucher saw the small blue numbers tattooed on his forearm, the indelible numbers the Nazis tattooed on the arms of Jews during World War II, designating a certain concentration camp. Or coke oven. Or soap factory. Or abattoir. Patiently Bucher waited until the enormous man's laughter subsided—already he was beginning to like Rabbi Levi Shimesh—then said:

"Kleyr told me you were born in America."

"That is correct, Mr. Bucher," the other said, wiping his eyes and still chuckling. "In Atlanta, Georgia, as a matter of fact, though if you don't detect a Southern accent it's because I haven't been back there in almost forty years now. I—" He stopped, pointing to the number tattooed on his forearm. "You noticed it a moment ago?"

Bucher nodded but said nothing.

"I was in Stuttgart, Germany visiting my older brother and his family in May of 1937. Hitler's Storm Troopers broke the doors in one night and hauled us off to prison. I never saw my brother or any of his family again."

"And they held you? An American?"

"Oh, yes. You see, the night the Storm Troopers came my passport, wallet, all my identification papers disappeared. Simply vanished. Oh, they pretended for a time to believe me when I told them I was an American citizen. But when they checked with German immigration they could find no record of my having entered the country; the records of my entry had also vanished, it seemed. So . . . I was sent to Bergen-Belsen, the concentration camp for dangerous political prisoners." He waved a baseball-glove-sized hand. "But that's history, Mr. Bucher. Right now we have a more pressing problem in the five kidnapped Jews—Mr. Bucher." He stopped, fixed Bucher with piercing eyes, heaved a tremendous sigh, and continued. "Mr. Bucher, I'm not sure I can prevent the JDL from attacking the Al

33

Fat'ha. And I'll be very honest with you; I'm not sure I want to. Thousands of years and millions of innocent people murdered for no other reason than the fact that they didn't believe in God as others thought—" The huge forefinger drumming the desk top was the only sound in the room. "My position as head of the Jewish Defense League is largely titular, Mr. Bucher. Nominal is a better word. I was asked to serve by the JDL's Steering Committee because the Steering Committee knows most of the JDL membership thinks the organization needs a man of my standing in the Jewish community to head the organization. But the Steering Committee runs the JDL, actually, and especially when things become as nitty-gritty as they are at present, because of the kidnappings."

"But the kidnappings weren't for nothing, Rabbi," Bucher said. "They took place for a reason, and the kidnappers may not know your position with the JDL is nominal; therefore, when there is a ransom demand made it is very likely to be made to you."

"Those kidnapped were Israeli citizens. Why would the kidnappers not make their ransom demands to the head of the Israeli mission to the UN?"

"Because the kidnappers aren't afraid of the Israeli mission to the United Nations, but they just might be afraid of the Jewish Defense League."

Rabbi Shimesh chuckled heartily. "They have good reason to fear the JDL, Mr. Bucher. The

34

militant membership of the organization is young men and women filled with the fire and spirit of freedom, young Americans who don't know how to crawl on their knees in servile submission as their forebears over the rest of the world did for centuries. Yes, I'd say the kidnappers have very good reason to fear the JDL. You mentioned Al Fat'ha. Are you of the mind that the Al Fat'ha is behind the kidnappings?"

"Who else?"

"That's a good question. Who else indeed?"

"Regardless, since you're thought to be the top man of the JDL, my guess is that the kidnappers will contact you first with their ransom demands."

The older man nodded slowly, thoughtfully. "I see . . . and perhaps you're right. And you want me to ask the JDL Steering Committee to keep the JDL in check. Is that it?"

"Will you do it?"

"Yes; but for how long, Mr. Bucher? Even the Steering Committee can't keep the militants restrained indefinitely. There are likely to be some who jump the traces as it is."

"Wait until the kidnappers make contact for the ransom. Then we'll put a time limit on it. Forty-eight hours should do it. Or seventy-two. Now . . ." Leaning forward to the desk, Bucher scribbled the telephone number of his suite at the Carlyle on a note pad. "If the kidnappers contact you, call this number and tell Kleyr. And

35

better speak in the old form of Hebrew. Just in case someone is listening in."

"You're not Jewish, Mr. Bucher, are you?"

"No."

"Then you're with the United States government?"

"No," Bucher lied evenly. "I'm not with the government."

"Then can you tell me why a Gentile is doing this for Jews?"

Bucher frowned in thought for a moment, then grinned engagingly. "So Kleyr and I can return to Puerto Rico and raise a family of twelve children."

"You're serious, aren't you?" There was the hint of amazement in Rabbi Levi Shimesh's rumble.

"Very serious—now, what can you tell me about Ahmed Fowzie?"

The older man shook his great, grizzled head.

"Nothing?" Bucher asked in dismay.

"That's right, Mr. Bucher. Absolutely nothing. The JDL has a crack intelligence unit, yet it has been unable to uncover a trace of Ahmed Fowzie's existence."

Bucher frowned in amazement. In so many words, it was the same answer he'd gotten from White Hat's director last night—nothing.

"Do you really intend to kill the man when, and if, you find him?" Rabbi Shimesh asked quietly.

"I sure as hell do. Troublemakers such as Ahmed Fowzie we can do without."

Silence. A long, heavy silence. It was the rabbi who broke it.

"In America today it is very simple for one to create for himself a completely new identity and to maintain this new identity as long as it does not come under careful scrutiny. Yet for one such as Ahmed Fowzie to be so—so public, as it were, so outspoken and active yet remain invisible and completely unknown—to me this seems impossible, Mr. Bucher, yet it is not impossible because it is happening. What are your thoughts on the matter?"

"You make it sound as if someone else is pretending to be Ahmed Fowzie," Bucher replied slowly.

"But why? To what end? For what purpose? The Ahmed Fowzies of this world don't act without motive."

"There's always money, and the Arabs have plenty."

"Ah, yes. They do that. At least the Mid-East Arabs do, and we're convinced they finance Al Fat'ha."

"Ahmed Fowzie is supposed to have cunningly outwitted the Jews in some way. How did he do it?"

"We don't know, Mr. Bucher. We don't even know what he is talking about. But shortly after I was elected to head the Jewish Defense League I denied it, whatever it is, during a TV interview and of course this convinced every Arab in the city it was true. Chalk one up for Ahmed Fowzie."

"Have you seen the plans for the hydrogen motor Nabil Chehade Shazar willed the American and Israeli Governments?"

"Oh, no. They're still held by probate court, I'm told, but I wouldn't see them in any event since I'm not an official of either government concerned." Rabbi Levi Shimesh chuckled heartily. "I'm also told that the Arab world went into a lather of distress when the story of the plans broke in the paper. Those Arabian oil kings see themselves losing billions in revenue from the sales of their overpriced black gold. I did hear the rumor, however, that the U.S. and Israel will offer to trade the Arab nations a franchise to build the hydrogen motor in return for a ten-year rollback in old prices to the 1935 level."

"They're tied together some way," Bucher said. "The plans for the hydrogen motor and the kidnappings, I mean."

The older man's chair groaned in protest when he came abruptly erect. "You think so?"

"I'm convinced of it. First the news story that Israel has a secret arsenal of ten atomic weapons of twenty-megaton power; the same as those the U.S. used in World War II; then the news story about the plans for building a hydrogen motor. My guess is that the Arabs aren't only in a lather of distress. They're desperate."

The older man combed huge fingers through his full beard, eyes focused on nothing and thinking hard. "By George," he said at last. "By George, you just might have something there, Mr. Bucher. The public kidnapping of the five Israeli UN members was an act of desperation if ever I've heard of one. . . ." His words trailed off and he continued to comb his beard. "But it's so incredibly stupid; the kidnappings. Assuming the Arabs committed the crime, and I'm convinced they did it. Still, I shouldn't be surprised. To paraphrase Gertrude Stein: an Arab is an Arab is an Arab."

"Meaning?" Bucher queried.

"You've been to the Middle East, Mr. Bucher?"

"Oh, yes. Several times."

"And did you not notice the difference between little Israel and the vast reaches of the Arabian world's endless deserts?"

Bucher nodded, understanding. Israel also had once been nothing but desert; yet, through its kibbutzim program, where once there was nothing but burning sand were now orchards, grain fields, rich pasturelands filled with fat herds, schools, hospitals, established communities any people could well be proud of—and the Arabs still had their sand, refusing, even, to learn the simple process of making fresh water of salty sea water, for which the Israeli government had volunteered to loan them technicians and engineers. For nothing. Simply as a good neighbor gesture. They had even refused the offer with a vulgar broadcast over Radio Cairo. "Yes, I agree," Bucher said. "An Arab is an Arab is an Arab." After a moment he continued, getting to his feet.

"Will you also ask the Jewish Defense League's intelligence unit to dig harder after Ahmed Fowzie?"

"I don't have to ask them, Mr. Bucher. They're digging, believe me. Not even the faintest hint of a clue to the man's identity and whereabouts goes ignored. I know. And if they uncover anything I'll call my little Puerto Rican genius at the number you gave me. Not that it'll give you a chance at Fowzie, Mr. Bucher. My guess is he'll be dead before even I learn he's been found. I suppose you're now going to see the Wog—Ali Annaser—to ask him to hold his Al Fat'ha in check and not attack the JDL just yet."

"That's my excuse for calling on the Wog, but I don't believe there's any danger of the Al Fat'ha attacking the JDL."

"You know," Rabbi Levi Shimesh mused as they shook hands, "I almost which they would."

Bucher was crossing the rabbi's tiny yard a minute later when the curtained black limousine purred past, the vehicle as out of place in the neighorhood as an udder on a bull, and as it did so, he looked straight into the cold, merciless eyes of the woman peeping at him, and at the rabbi's house behind him, through the small part she held in the rear curtain. Recognition was instantaneous, both for Bucher and for the woman. He saw it reflect in her startled eyes.

"I be goddamn," he muttered, a bit surprised

40

to find one of the doxies who'd hustled in Winston-Salem for the Syndicate when he was crime overlord of the organization's East Coast Division cruising about New York in a curtained, chauffeured limousine. The vehicle was not one of the city's many limousines available for rental. This he determined from the license plate. The car was a privately owned vehicle, though whether it belonged to . . . He frowned, trying to remember the woman's name—not the name she had used in hustling, but her real name. It was not a really common name as he recalled, yet neither was it sufficiently uncommon to be rare or outstanding. Keepler? No. that wasn't it. Heelpler? Delpler? Deepleer? Beepler? Beeplor? *Maud!* That was it! Her first name, anyway. Maud—Maud—Maud Ann—*Beeker!* By God that was *it!* Maud Ann Beeker. She'd started as a trollop at age thirteen. On the streets of Winston-Salem, North Carolina. Got picked up and jailed by the cops half a dozen times before an older doxy wised her up and she'd come to him, asking for a place in one of the houses he controlled. And he'd given her a place. Her youth mattered nothing. Not with the grease he'd laid out for protection each week. Maud Ann Beeker . . . Bucher shook his head in wonder at seeing her again, today, in a limousine. Though it shouldn't surprise him. Even as a kid of thirteen she'd been tough and mean and hard as nails, one of the climbers, one of those who meant to get ahead, to make it rich come hell or high water. If he were to believe his eyes, Maud Ann Beeker had made it for sure—assuming it had been her limousine she was riding in. Let's see—Bucher frowned in concentration, figuring the woman's age. Christ! She'd come to him approximately fifteen years ago, so Maud Ann Beeker wasn't even thirty years old yet. Or even twenty-nine, for that matter. Nor had the face he'd seen in the limousine looked any older, or even that old, for if he remembered correctly she had been one of those rare females who literally thrived on prostitution. Loved every minute of it.

New York has two Greenwich Villages, one the villagers' Village, the other the tourists' Village. The former, where the real villagers live, work, and frolic, in general is an area west of Seventh Avenue that is a veritable jumble of streets with such names as Perry, Barrow, Morton, Charles, Bedford, and the like. In this area the coffee houses are not jammed together side by side, nor are the streets glaring with neon at every passer-by, and it contains the oldest and the quaintest houses in Greenwich Village. It also contains roaring cafes without a sign or anything else out front save a plain, unadorned door to indicate their existence, and it is in these that the verbally vociferous and the cause- and philosophy-dedicated true bohemians hold forth in happy, boisterous disputations. The other Village, since it is the tourists' Village, is highly commercialized, the streets lined with bookstalls, health food shops, wine shops, basket weavers, leather workers, plus more nightclubs featuring jazz and folk singers, more coffee houses, and more off-Broadway theaters than any other area in New York City.

The tourists' Village was Bucher's destination; specifically, the off-Broadway theater called 99 Names. He found it on Bleecker Street—the name of the street reminding him again of Maud Ann Beeker—three blocks from the famous Circle in the Square Theatre, between an art gallery and a pornography shop. He had not expected 99 Names to be open at this early hour of the morning, nor was he disappointed.

The marquee of 99 Names showed a lone Arab on a lone camel, with flecks of paint beginning to peel from both. "Hey, buddy. Can you spare a dollar for a cup of coffee?" The coarse, gravelly voice of the man speaking from behind Bucher caused him to turn quickly from the large double doors of 99 Names.

The speaker's cast-off woolen coat hung almost to his knees; the sleeves had been hacked off, apparently, with a hatchet or a large knife and left unhemmed, and his ancient trousers, once a robin's-egg blue, were now the hue of skimmed milk into which curds of soot had been stirred. One of his shoes was a black and white oxford, the other a heavy work brogan, neither of more recent vintage than his coat and pants. The speaker himself was small, approaching middle age, and, due to body heat accumulated under the heavy, out-of-season woolen coat, perspiration streamed down his face, which he mopped repeatedly with a large blue bandana. He was White Hat.

Bucher's granite features gave no hint of recognition as he handed the other a dollar, though a quiet chuckle accompanied the words when he spoke. "What the hell are you doing here, Neuf? And what happened to your French accent?"

"Here in America I file the accent away for only occasional use," the other said, speaking and gesturing in a manner that anyone watching would think was a plea for more money. "As for my being here, in the Village, I've been waiting for you to appear. The Old Man wants you to call him."

Bucher nodded. "Old Man" was Neuf's reference to White Hat's director. "What about?"

"This morning you weren't where you told him last night you would be, apparently. From what I gather. And something big has come up."

"Like what?"

"That I was not told. But the Old Man insists that it is of the utmost importance that you call him quickly. He summoned me at once on learning you were not registered at the New York Hilton."

"So why that getup you're wearing?" Neuf, high-ranking officer of French national security, was in the States as a guest-student of White Hat's operational techniques.

"Because," Neuf told him, "of the five kidnapped Jews. I am French. The Old Man suspects the Arabs are behind the kidnappings. The French and the Arabs have a long history of togetherness, especially in Africa. Not always peaceful togetherness, but togetherness nonetheless, and this 99 Names theater is headquarters for the Al Fat'ha. The Old Man thought I might be able to inveigle my way into their good graces if I came down here and made like a tramp."

"Have you learned anything?"

"Nothing," the smaller man said. "Except that there's a back door to the theater. Go down the alley on the far side of the porn shop and turn left; the door has a large red garbage can on each side of it and—" The smaller man stopped abruptly, a coup d'oeil and suddenly frantic gestures warning Bucher. "Aw, come on, buddy," Neuf whined servilely, holding a palm upward beseechingly. "Another buck, huh? Just one more? Ain't nobody can buy nothing these days for only one, and—"

"Beat it, bum!" Bucher snarled in the other's face, whispering: "What the hell is it?"

"Move out," Neuf replied in kind. "Separate." This he followed by more gestures and a louder, keener whine.

Bucher turned brusquely and walked toward the porn shop. But he did not enter the shop. Instead, he stopped in front of the shop's right window, about to surreptitiously case the scene behind him, wondering at the cause of Neuf's sudden change, when he noted in the shop's window the reflection of a long, black limousine cruising past. Not wanting to turn too quickly and thereby attract attention to himself, he waited a couple of seconds before looking after the vehicle, which was identical to the one he had earlier seen driving past Rabbi Shimesh's battered home. But he turned too late to get the license number was therefore unable to determine if it was the limousine in which he had seen Maud Ann Beeker. But why the devil would Maud Ann Beeker have trailed him all the way to Greenwich Village? To what purpose? For old times' sake? Bucher doubted this. She was not the type. Also, he could not be certain the limousine was the same in which he had seen the woman—which, Bucher decided after some seconds, was a bit much to be mere coincidence. There were literally hundreds of long, black limousines in New York. Bucher at last decided the vehicle must be one of those instead of the one he'd seen earlier; he glanced toward the spot in front of the 99 Names theater where he had left Neuf. The little Frenchman was nowhere in sight.

Bucher found the rear entrance of 99 Names easily, and it was exactly as Neuf had described it; there was a large red trash barrel on each side of the door that opened off the alley at ground level. His hope was to enter the place unnoticed and give it a thorough shakedown, and he was reaching for the knob to determine if the rear entrance was locked when he noticed the door was ajar. Not much. No more than one-sixteenth of an inch. But ajar nonetheless. Cautiously he retreated a step to one side, then gently thrust against the door with a forefinger. With modified inner-sanctum sounds of protest the door slowly swung inward onto a wide and dim hallway leading toward the building's interior. The hallway was unadorned save by a wooden box the size and shape of a dynamite box, the box unadorned save by an Arab lad the size and shape of age ten, the lad adorned by Mets T-shirt, jeans, and white tennis shoes. His large and limpid eyes studied Bucher solemnly against the lighter background of the day outside, his whole self revealing that he considered his function as sentry of no small moment.

"Are you Mr. Tony Pelegroso of Chicago?" the boy asked Bucher respectfully, rising to attention.

"Hey," Bucher said in tones of apology but wondering what the Al Fat'ha wanted with Tony Pelegroso, ace triggerman from Chicago. "I didn't mean to keep a good soldier waiting at his post." At the word "soldier" the boy straightened further, his zeal tilting him backward. Bucher fished a five spot from his pocket and tucked it in the neck of the lad's T-shirt. "That's just between us fellows," he said, speaking as one man to another. "But that traffic this morning was unbelievable." He winked in great camaraderie. "Now if you'll show me to the way to go . . ."

Bucher's spontaneous stratagem produced quick results. Without warning, childish exuberance overcame the lad and he dashed down the hall, shrieking at the top of his young voice to Ali

47

Annaser that Mr. Tony Pelegroso of Chicago had arrived.

Bucher followed at once without bothering to close the door, though unable to keep up with the youngster without undue haste. Even so, he encountered no difficulty in finding his way. At the far end of the broad hallway an equally broad passage led past the open door of a huge prop room and several much smaller rooms which, Bucher assumed, were dressing rooms for actors appearing in 99 Names productions. Partway down this second hallway the faintly nauseating odor of spoiling mutton smote him across the face, and as he progressed the odor commingled with that of curry, overcooked chupatties, anise, plus others unidentified odors, all of which resulted in a smell that would gag a hog. Bucher slowed so his nostrils would become used to the stench, and he succeeded, although once his stomach bucked threateningly in protest.

The double doors at the end of the second passage were as wide as the passage itself, Bucher soon discovered why. The answer was in the form of a man. The Wog, no less. Ali Annaser. A minimum width of five feet was required of doors before the Wog, veritably a small mountain of greasy, sweating, malodorous suet, could pass from one room to another. Bucher saw him first in the huge kitchen behind the double doors, which were propped wide, laboring over a hot stove, assaulting the contents of an enormous pot with an equally enormous spoon. Of the lad who had

48

been waiting for Tony Pelegroso there was no sign; he had already gone to invest the five dollars Bucher had given him in such childish delights as candy, gum, carbonated beverages, and other such readily available commodities that rot the teeth and damage the kidneys. The greasy mountain of malodorous suet maneuvered itself to face Bucher's direction, beaming servilely.

"Dear Mr. Pelegroso," he burpled oilily, waddle-rolling toward Bucher, hand extended in greeting. "So good of you to come, dear sir—pray forgive this frightful mess." His vague gesture indicated the entire kitchen, and it was here that Bucher saw the source of the rotting mutton stench: the maggot-infested hind quarters of a sheep in a garbage can beside the door, a huge red can similar to the two bracketing the outside door. "The great Ahmed Fowzie insisted that I keep our negotiations with you strictly business, ha, ha, but—perhaps a platter of succulent young lamb with coos-coos and—"

Bucher's tone in replying projected the Hollywood concept of the underworld archgoon: "I never eat when I'm working. Bad for the indigestation."

Ali Annaser, thinking himself in the presence of one of Chicago's legendary professional killers —as Bucher knew first-hand Tony Pelegroso to be—shivered visibly in perverse ecstasy. And grinned.

"My god a'mighty," Bucher thought at the sight of the other's grin; it split the Wog's face from

49

ear to ear. "This sonofabitch could swallow base-balls without half trying." It was the biggest mouth Bucher had ever seen on a human being.

"Let us adjourn to the theater proper," Annaser said in greasy grandiloquence. "In an area to the right of the stage the furniture is more accom-modating."

Bucher was unable to understand this last until they emerged into the theater and, to the right, he saw what appeared to be a chair-shaped bench but which, he soon learned, was merely a chair, massively built of stout woods and metal and large enough to accommodate Ali Annaser's vast pos-terior. Numerous wooden chairs of normal size and varying designs sat haphazardly about. Be-yond and to one side were the seats of the theater, sufficient to handle no more than two hundred, Bucher estimated, while behind and to their rear was the stage which, despite the small audience capacity, was enormous.

"It affords the astute director, such as I, the opportunity of infinite variety," Annaser oozed when he noticed Bucher casing the stage.

"And the speakers?" Bucher asked.

"For effects, especially when the scene demands whispered dialogue. They're very useful then."

"Yeah," Bucher replied with total disinterest, straddling one of the wooden chairs and facing Annaser, for the first time realizing the man's eyes could not be seen, sunken as they were in caves of fat. "So what's this you want with me?"

The other affected surprise. "Were you not told

50

the nature of the job before leaving Chicago?"

"You're goddamn right I was told, fatso,"
Bucher snarled in unmistakable menace. "But I
was told on the phone. Now I want it from you
or no dice, see? So if I get the wrong info and
things goof on me, I'll know where to find at
least a part of the cause, meaning *you*, fatso!"
After some seconds' pause, during which the Wog
sat with maw agape in fear, Bucher continued
in a conciliatory tone, wondering if he had
overplayed his role as Tony Pelegroso. "You see,
friend," he said, making gestures with both
hands. "In my—er—business we don't have insurance and things like that, see? When we—when
I go do a piece of work, either it gets done good
or it don't get done good. If it's good, then I
walk away fine and dandy. But if I do the job
I contracted to do but don't walk away safe and
clear, then it ain't good, see? So far all of my jobs
have been done good on account of I make certain
I understand all angles of it; so now you tell me
face to face like, huh?" Bucher winked in com-
radely fashion. "I do this job good and maybe
you'll be wanting others done also. Get it?"

The sigh of a ruptured gas bag escaped Wog
Annaser; his relief was almost visible. "There is
a man in New York who is making a nuisance of
himself, Mr. Pelegroso. We—my organization, the
Al Fat'ha, want you to take care of this man for
us."

"You mean knock him off," Bucher said. "You
want me to give the guy the rub."

51

Annaser's neckless head nodded sagely, his terraced chins quivering judiciously with the gravity of the moment.

"That's the way I got it," Bucher continued. "Only my people in Chi didn't identify the mark. He gotta name?"

"They call him the Butcher."

4

"Well, now," Bucher beamed engagingly, in no wise surprised. "This gets more interesting by the second. The Butcher, huh? Jeeeez, I been waiting a long time for a crack at him."

"You know him?" the Wog asked in a mixture of admiration and fear.

"Know him? Hell, yes I know him! We grew up together, you might say. In Chi." Abruptly Bucher jabbed the air with a forefinger several times in the other's direction. "I get the Syndicate's dead-only hit price on the Butcher's head, understand?"

"Hit price? What hit price? The Al Fat'ha's giving you thirty thou—"

"Half now." Bucher swung a hand toward Wog Annaser, palm up. "Fifteen thousand now and half when the job is done. I goof and the other half goes to my boss in Chi. And if I goof and you welch on the second fifteen thou, some of my friends in Chi'll be making A-rab stew outta you." This last, apparently, inclined the fat man not to pursue the subject of the Syndicate's hit price on Bucher's head, for he dug vigorously beneath the folds of the vast robe he wore and came forth with a thick stack of hundred-dollar bills.

"There are one hundred and fifty of them there," he told Bucher while handing him the bills. "Count them if you like."

"Not necessary," Bucher said expansively, stowing the bills inside his shirt. "You gotta trust the people you do business with or it sours up things. Now, where do I find ol' Butcher-boy?"

"I'm not sure," the Wog said slowly. "Ahmed Fowzie's people lost him last night in the vicinity of the Carlton Hotel; he's not registered at the Carlton. That's certain. We've checked." He produced pad and pen from somewhere on his person and extended them to Bucher. "But we are planning a trap for the Butcher here at 99 Names and setting it with bait he cannot resist, so if you'll leave me a number, when the trap is ready I'll give you a ring. Then you come here, do what you're paid to do—in front of witnesses who will never be able to identify you later, I might add—collect the remainder of your fee, and return to Chicago."

Bucher feigned astonished delight. "And that's all?"

"That's all, Mr Pelegroso." Again the Wog grinned; from corner to corner his mouth would have measured at least eight inches. Hastily Bucher scribbled a White Hat blind telephone number on the pad—he would receive with all possible dispatch any information called in to the number—and gave pad and pen back to the Wog.

"My private phone service here in New York," he chuckled suggestively, implying the fat man would understand him, then said: "My people would like to meet your Ahmed Fowzie."

In the midst of a compliant snigger, the gargoyle-like obscenity that was the Wog's face changed into a mask of speculative cunning.

"Why?" he wheezed.

"Business, dammit. Thirty thousand dollars for a hit is not bad profit. We could use a lot of 'em in Chi." He chanced a blind shot in the dark. "Me and Maud Ann."

"Maud Ann?"

"Maud Ann Beeker—friend of mine. You wouldn't know her." Bucher held his breath, but to no avail. The blind shot went wild, didn't pay off. He got to his feet, continuing: "Call that number I gave you when you're ready for me to burn the Butcher. Say when and where. I'll handle the how."

The other struggled, gasping and puffing, to his feet also. "Oh, it'll be right here at 99 Names, Mr. Pelegroso. You can depend on that. As I said, we'll set the trap for this Butcher with bait he can't refuse. Oh, yes. You can depend on earning

55

your fee right here at this theater, for the Butcher
will be here."

Bucher departed the same way he had arrived,
but at the open door of the prop room he stopped,
sniffing inquisitively, frowning in reflection. Although his nose was used to the foul smells emanat-
ing from the kitchen, he now detected a totally
new smell, that of hashish and zibeeb, this latter
a potent Arabian liqueur held by many to contain
the properties of an aphrodisiac. Again he sniffed
experimentally, trying to locate the source of this
new smell, all the while cudgeling his memory in
an attempt to recall where he had recently, very
recently in fact, noted the identical odor. When
memory failed to respond—Bozeman's Bar!
That's where he's smelled it! Last night in Curdi's
Crudhouse! By the toenails of God—!

And yet—what relevance did the odor of hashish and zibeeb in the 99 Names theater have to
the kidnapping of the five members of the Israeli
mission to the United Nations? Or to the odor
having been in Bozeman's Bar last night, for
that matter? Bucher was well on his way to Bozeman's bar when these things occurred to him.
And before he remembered Neuf's message from
White Hat's director; he would call the director
from the bar. Moreover, after Ali Annaser had
time to discover the mistake of assuming him to
be Tony Pelegroso, he would return to the 99
Names and put the obscenely obese sonofabitch
under pressure to reveal the location where the

five Israelis were held captive. Bucher was only blocks from Bozeman's Bar, however, before he spotted his tail—a green Volks bug that had done a remarkable job of deception by remaining concealed in traffic. When he parked near the bar the small vehicle shot past, the young woman behind the wheel casting not so much as a fleeting glance in his direction.

Bucher entered Bozeman's Bar by the front door and found the place as empty as it had been the night before, Boze Curdi behind the bar exuding unvarnished timidity and nervous apprehension by each gesture he made, each look he gave, each breath he took.

"Jesus!" Bucher thought, but not without sympathy. Any man who'd fall as hard for a woman as Boze had fallen for his dancer-wife, ex-wife she was now, might best go lie on the beach somewhere for a few months and ponder the inevitability of it all. Years ago in the Syndicate, and before he'd met and married Lorili Popjoy Lamour, Boze Curdi had been a real man, not what Bucher would term as overly bright in the think-department, but a real man nonetheless. Bucher had never seen Lorili Popjoy Lamour, wouldn't know the woman if he bumped into her on the street, nor did he want to. Any woman who wrecked the life of any man the way she had wrecked Boze Curdi's could be compared only with the black widow spider, and such women were better shunned.

Bucher took the same seat at the bar that he

had occupied the night before and curled a finger in command for Boze Curdi to draw near, which Curdi was already doing, clean glass in one hand, bottle of Johnny Walker Red in the other.

"Hold it, Boze." Bucher covered the glass with a hand when Curdi set it on the bar. "No Scotch this time. Zibeeb."

"Zibeeb, Bucher?" Curdi's tone implied he doubted his ears.

"Right. Zibeeb."

Curdi's jaw went slack and he scratched behind an ear, a feeble-simple grin flicking across his washed-out features. "You putting me on, Bucher. I don't know how to mix a zibeeb. You're the first customer I ever had that asked for one."

"It's not a mixed drink, Boze," Bucher said patiently. "It's an Arabian liqueur. Like anisette, only much stronger, and heavily perfumed."

Curdi turned, leaning with both hands against the edge of the bar, and eyeballed the shelved rows of bourbons, Scotches, ryes, corn, gins, vermouths, wines, but all domestic. No zibeeb.

"Bucher, I'm sorry," he whined, facing across the bar again, "but we ain't got it. There is a local who comes in here sometimes; he was in here last night. Early. A bit before you showed. And he drinks a weird mixture like you said, all perfumed and all, but he always brings his own bottle. And I let him. He never causes any trouble. Just sits 'way back there in that back booth, drinking his stuff and smoking. Best customer I got, really.

58

He always gives me ten dollars just to come in and sit and smoke—"

"What?"

"Huh?"

"What does he smoke?"

Bozeman Curdi withered inside. It showed in his eyes, the look of a dog caught sucking eggs. His voice held a noticeable tremor when he continued in a furtive whisper. "Bucher, I ain't got many regulars, mostly walk-ins off the street and usually they're boys I used to know on skid row. And rent on this dump is—"

"Hashish?" Bucher asked. "Is that what the mutt smokes? Hashish?"

"Bucher—"

"Have you forgotten who you're talking to? You think I'd run and squeal to the cops? Me?"

Boze Curdi stared fixedly at Bucher a moment, then nodded doggedly. "Yeah," he said. "The guy smokes hash."

"What's he look like?"

"Medium, sort of, fair skin and dirty blond hair. Always wears a turtleneck sweater. I don't know his name." He moved to the sink under the bar and commenced washing glasses noisily, and Bucher sat with a sinking feeling in the pit of his stomach.

He had been mistaken in thinking there might be some connection between the odor of zibeeb and hash at 99 Names theater and the same odor here at Bozeman's Bar. It was nothing more than a rare coincidence, for certainly the man Boze had described was no Arab. Still . . .

"What happened to the creep who got himself bumped here last night, Boze?"

"I called the cops, like you said to, and they come and took the body away and when they asked me how it happened I told them the guy was trying to rob me, like you said, and you shot him. That satisfied them, but I expect they'll be back later."

"Yeah." Bucher knew they would not be back. White Hat would make certain the death of the apish goon Kleyr had deep-sixed would get little notice.

Boze Curdi continued to wash glasses at such a high level of noise neither he nor Bucher at first noticed the newcomer, though she entered the bar with no apparent attempt at keeping her presence unknown, for the moment her eyes fell on Bucher she cried: "Darling!" in a smoky contralo that sent pleasurable squiggles trickling over his spine and dashed toward him, arms spread—almost identical to the way Kleyr Boriquen had arrived the night before. The young woman wore knit jeans of small gray-green checks and a jacket to match, the garments accentuating the small waist, the curvesome hips, and the aggressively forward-thrusting breasts. She flung herself bodily at Bucher; he caught her, holding on and keeping them both erect with difficulty as she commenced smothering him with kisses, in the process managing the barely audible whisper:

"Tony Pelegroso followed you from 99 Names. He's coming here now."

Bucher eased back from her, was about to ask: "Who're you?" when his gaze fell on the small gold pendant in the Star of David design suspended from her neck and instead asked:

"JDL?"

"Uh-huh. Sharon Szold."

Bucher stared. "The singer . . . ? The Golden Songbird?" Recently he'd read in a national news magazine that there was scarcely a jukebox in the country that did not have at least one record by Sharon Szold, the Golden Songbird.

"Surprise, Mr. Bucher." She withdrew a step, her throaty laughter hititing him low and on the inside.

"I see. But you also shadow itinerant gunsels in green Volks bugs."

"Rabbi Shimesh though you might need help." At his quick doubletake she laughed again, "Oh, I do things besides sing, Mr. Bucher. Such as—" She took one of his hands in hers, closed down on it, and despite the great difference in size between his hand and hers Bucher was forced to exert himself against her grip. "—teach judo, karate, and other systems of self-defense three times a week to JDL girls."

"I bet your husband lives in broken-bone casts."

"I'm not married—yet. But I'm looking. And I've already put Kleyr Boriquen on notice—" She burst into happy laughter at his flabbergasted expression.

"You know Kleyr?" he managed oafishly.

"Everybody knows Kleyr, everybody in the New York Jewish community, as the *Times* labels all Jews living in New—"

"Hold it. We've got company. Move aside."

Tony Pelegroso stood just inside the front door. He was fortyish, well over six feet, but lean and lanky, seldom tipping the scales above one-sixty. His swarthy face was deeply scarred by acne and his dress was impeccable: black alligator Bengal chukkas, gentle blue open-weave vicuña sport coat with custom tailored slacks a shade darker and, like Al Capone, he favored shirts of white on white. He was Italian, and had been christened Antonio Giovanni Tucheti, the family name of which Chicago's ribald Irish youth bastardized into an expression derived from a four-letter word common in circles scatological and which was preceded by the adverb "too." Tony Tucheti years later avenged himself by financing his name-change to Pelegroso with money he took from an Irishman after he had slit the man's gullet, never suspecting that his new name was no more Italian than Tucheti had been French.

"Butcher," Pelegroso said in pseudo-friendly fashion. "You ain't changed a lot since our days together in Chicago."

"Neither have you, Tony," Bucher replied effortlessly, standing alone now, with a quick flick of his hand motioning Sharon Szold farther aside. "You're still the same ignorant, stupid, unwashed son of a bitch you were then. You come here to take me, punk? Then make your bid, you creepy bastard."

All pretense of camaraderie vanished from Pelegroso's bony countenance. He stared at the man facing him. For reasons he could not readily recall, since accepting the Al Fat'ha's contract to kill Bucher he had become of the mind that Bucher feared him and his fearsome reputation.

"You latched onto my trail at the 99 Names theater?" Bucher asked the killer from Chicago.

"I phoned Annaser from a joint near there and he filled me in on the way you'd shook him down for fifteen Gs making like you was me and all. Musta made you feel real big, imitating Tony Pelegroso."

"To begin with, you're nothing but a damn imitation—friend Tucheti." Despite the presence of Sharon Szold, Bucher's pronunciation of the man's former family name smacked far more of Chicago ribald Irish than it did of the correct Italian. "And I got the fifteen Gs on me now. They're yours if you can take them."

"Oh, I'll take 'em easy enough. The way I got it, you're running mostly to bluff these days. Gone soft, like. Ain't the real dreadful badass you was in the old days."

"How would you like a deal, Tony?" A proposition germinating among Bucher's thoughts since Pelegroso's arrival had a moment past blossomed into full acceptance.

"What sort of deal?" The man was edgy.

"A hundred thousand dollars, cash, and a

guaranteed safe return to Chicago in exchange for the address of Ahmed Fowzie."

Now seated in the end booth of the row of booths lining the wall across the room from the bar, Sharon Szold watched the one-time Syndicate crime overlord and the professional hit man from Chicago come to kill him with considerably more than casual interest. To her, life-and-death drama was no stranger, though here in America she knew it less first-hand than as a heritage; yet, from the First Captivity thousands of years ago to Hitler's mass family-murder chambers and the factories for converting Jews into soap in Nazi Germany, and now to this new form of Arab Nazism, the history of her people was one grueling, never-ceasing, life-and-death drama centered around a struggle for survival. Perhaps it was because of this that she could fully appreciate the casual indifference underlying Bucher's gutsy attitude.

A direct result of this heritage of struggle for survival was Sharon Szold's instinctive, unconscious preparation to join Bucher against this hired killer from Chicago. To remain a spectator safely on the sideline no more occurred to her than did flapping her arms and trying for the moon. He was fighting for her and her people and therefore would not fight alone. Killer Pelegroso's unusually loud tone interrupted her thoughts.

"And that's all? A hundred Gs for Ahmed Fowzie's address?" Pelegroso's voice crackled with excitement.

"That's all," Bucher replied evenly. "Only don't pick any address out of the air and claim it's Fowzie's. To insure against this, you remain in New York with some of my people until I burn Fowzie."

"Whaddaya mean, your people?" He squinted suspiciously.

"I don't mean your stinking Arabs. Do we deal?"

Pelegroso remained fixed in place, moving not a muscle, for so long Bucher was about to repeat the question, when slowly he shook his head.

"Huh-uh. No deal. A hundred Gs ain't near like the two hundred eighty I get from the Syndicate and the Al Fat'ha for burning you."

"Just as I figured." A throaty snarl accompanied Bucher's words. "You don't know where Fowzie is. Chances are you've never seen the crut."

"Ain't nobody ever seen him." Pelegroso's bony face was sullen with hatred because Bucher had pinpointed his reason for refusing the hundred thousand dollars.

"Nobody? Not even Ali Annaser?"

"I said nobody!"

"Mr. Bucher." Sharon Szold rose gracefully to her feet. "If you and this distinguished gentleman have no objection I think I'll go. My children are waiting in the station wagon and I left the windows up. And in this heat . . ." As Sharon was talking, she was moving toward the front door and Tony Pelegroso who, for reasons known only to those who understand the mental processes of depraved killers, chose that particular instant to go for his .357 snub-nose revolver. In a move more instinctive than conscious, Sharon, within two steps of the man, flattened against the wall and out of the line of fire when he whipped the revolver up—

"Koosh!"

The gentle death sigh of the silencered Walther P-38 that appeared in Bucher's big hand sounded loud in the hush that preceded by a heartbeat the rattle of Pelegroso's weapon against the floor, and by a heartbeat and a half Pelegroso's profane exclamation of dismay and chagrin as he lobbed bodily through the air in Bucher's direction.

A whimper of terror escaped Bozeman Curdi, who cringed behind the bar, as Pelegroso's five-point landing on knees, elbows, and face half a dozen yards in front of where a surprised Bucher stood rattled a window somewhere in the building. Wild-eyed, Pelegroso had scrambled halfway erect when Sharon's foot reached the end of a powerful swing against his unprotected, protruding chin with bone-crushing force. Again Pelegroso took to the airways, this time straight up to shoulder height, where he flattened out, face up and horizontal, and crashed to the floor a second time. Again somewhere a window rattled. Bending over to seize the addled killer by nape and seat, Sharon Szold looked around and winked enormously at Bucher.

"You want to pitch him around some?"

"You need help?" Bucher suspected his question was superfluous as he asked it, and saw proof of this a second later when Tony Pelegroso's trajectory carried the man to the far wall, off which he bounced with many grunts and sobs.

"Never," Sharon grinned engagingly. "I told you I teach karate and judo. The question is: what do we do with this thing?" She straightened and whirled, her graceful body snapping forward powerfully in the process, and this time Pelegroso richocheted off the wall at a keen angle, careened around the phone booth, struck the floor shoulders first, and lay still. Bucher looked at the cringing Curdi, then pointed to the phone behind the bar.

"Call the cops, Boze. Tell them Pelegroso is guilty of killing a clerk at the Safeway Finance Company in Evanston, Illinois in . . . in . . ." Bucher frowned, remembering hard. "Eleven years ago last March. Okay?" He watched Curdi scuttle to the phone crabwise, seemingly unable to take his eyes off the downed killer, Bucher then thumbed a dime into the public phone recently assaulted by Pelegroso and dialed the number where he knew White Hat's director to be. When the line clicked alive from the other end, because of Sharon Szold's presence, he resorted to a long-dead Serbo-Croatian dialect.

"This is the Iceman."

A hushed pause followed; then White Hat's director's voice came on the wire, also speaking in Serbo-Croatian, which did not conceal the tense alarm underlying his tone.

"Mr. Bucher, three bandits of Arab nationality, each armed with a powerful rifle fitted with telescopic sights, have barricaded themselves on the roof of the Secretariat Building at United Nations Headquarters in what they claim is a battle-to-the-death protest of Israel's being willed plans for the hydrogen motor by Nabil Chehade Shazar. They demanded that a copy of the plans be delivered to them."

"So give 'em a copy of plans—of the engine in Henry Ford's first Model T. Ignorant-assed Arabs won't know the difference."

"But the bandits demand that the plans be delivered to them by the U.S. Secretary of State —which the President will never agree to—who is then to remain in their custody until qualified scientists of their selection have verified the plans are of Shazar's hydrogen motor."

"How high is the UN's Secretariat Building?"

"Five hundred and fifty feet—thirty-nine stories; and we can't clear the area and starve them out if that's what you're thinking, for they have with them one of the building's security guards, whom they swear they will throw off the top of the Secretariat if their demands are not met by sundown."

Bucher stared some seconds at the phone in his hand, knowing he had heard correctly. "Jesus James H. Christ," he at last intoned absently. Then: "So what do you plan on doing?"

"I've just done it," the director said, unable to

keep all the self-dissatisfaction from his tone. "I've just passed the buck to you."

"What?"

"I'm sorry, Mr. Bucher. I'm Sam White, not Harry Truman. It's your baby. None of the news media has glommed onto the thing yet; the bandits had a kid with them as messenger and sent him to the UN Security Chief with their demands. He contacted the FBI, who in turn contacted us."

"Why the hell didn't the FBI carry the ball?" Bucher demanded harshly.

"They will if the story of the situation breaks to the public, but because of possible international complications, the President wants us to handle the thing. As private citizens."

Bucher could not resist: "I believe by God you're serious."

"Mr. Bucher . . ." The pleading in the older man's voice was unmistakable.

"Okay. Okay. But at times like this I always remember life in the Syndicate as the good ol' days. Hang on a sec." Bucher frowned at the floor in deep thought, remembering that the UN's Secretariat Building was bounded on the east by the East River, with only the four-story Conference Building separating it from the water . . . hummm . . . if he had . . . hummm . . . perhaps if he took a . . . Jesus! One tiny wrong move and he'd be cold meat. So . . . "Okay," he said aloud into the phone. "I'll be there soon as I can make it. In the meantime, here's a list of items, and people, you can herd together." He called off the things on his hastily constructed mental list slowly, often resorting to English due to the paucity of technical terms in the Serbo-Croatian dialect, at last concluding with: "Got it?"

At the director's affirmative grunt he hung up, thumbed a second dime into the phone, and dialed his suite at the Carlyle Hotel. When Kleyr failed to answer by the tenth ring, he again hung up the phone; perhaps she was in the bath, or, since she was to remain in the suite until White Hat got this Jew-Arab-United Nations hassle settled, she may have gone back to bed after his departure. Regardless, he'd call again from White Hat headquarters, his immediate destination.

"Hey! Not so fast! I'm still here, remember?" Sharon Szold stood near the unconscious figure of Tony Pelegroso, open palms extended in a "how come?" gesture.

"Sorry." Bucher turned at the front entrance. "This next job I do alone." She moved toward him as he spoke. "Tell Rabbi Shimesh to keep a tight rein on the JDL; something may be about to break in our favor." He hoped this last wasn't the lie he suspected it to be. "Can we keep in touch?" He laughed shortly. "In case another Chicago gunsel comes looking for me?"

"You're sure I can't accompany you?" She clearly wanted to do so; it showed in her eyes.

"It can't happen." Bucher shook his head in finality. "Not this time."

"You can reach me through the JDL, or Rabbi Shimesh's phone, or—" She scribbled hastily on the back of a bar coaster. "—at this number. At my home. And especially call my home number if you ever need the services of an expert aerodynamist."

"What?" Bucher stared at the famous vocalist in honest surprise. Included in the list he had called over the phone to White Hat's director was an aerodynamics engineer.

"I heard you mention 'aerodynamics engineer' on the phone. It sounds almost the same in whatever language, and my brother David has been in the theory and research division of Rhodes Aircraft for years."

"I be goddamn," Bucher intoned flatly in characteristic fashion. "Can you get him? I mean can your brother leave his job for a few hours?"

Sharon Szold nodded eagerly. "He's head of the division."

"Come on." Bucher wheeled toward the door. We'll take your bug. It's faster through traffic than the Olds."

Two hours later, two hours of frenzied activity in the sub-basement of an unimpressive brick building on Central Park West, Bucher, White Hat's director, Sharon Szold, David Szold, and a twenty-member gaggle of White Hat technicians, stood around the giant sky sail of unique, even radical, design.

"To be certain of the craft it should be tested, Mr. Bucher." David Szold, approaching middle age, had thick, grayish hair tending to wave, a

71

wide, powerful body and, to Bucher his most noticeable feature, the strong, sensitive hands of a concert violinist. Under his direction the sky sail had literally blossomed into being. On arrival, both he and his famous sister were taken aside by Sam White, made aware of the situation, and asked for their pledge of silence regarding their participation in the matter, with both complying without hesitation.

"There's no time to test the craft," Bucher said to the gathering at large. "Disassemble and pack it. We're short of time." He turned to Sam White. "I need to huddle with the one that tows me. Who's the pilot?"

"I am," the director said somewhat testily. "Since you've decided on suicide I'll not go *fainéant*. I want to see you go out in a blaze of glory with all the grace and flair possible."

5

Bucher ignored the director's comments, knowing the older man was angry with himself for having been responsible for placing one of his agents in a situation wherein chances of survival were practically nil.

"Let's take another look at the blowup," Bucher said. "David, will you join us?"

The blowup, leaning against the far wall, was a sixteen-by-twenty-foot enlargement of an aerial photograph of the United Nations Secretariat, General Assembly, Conference, and Library buildings, and also included a stretch of the East River, the two residental-commercial towers just north of UN Headquarters at 866 United Nations Plaza and, most important to Bucher, the bridges spanning the East River beyond the two towers.

"There." Bucher pointed to the bridges. "Going under them at two hundred miles an hour is where the hassle begins."

"May I accompany you in the tow-plane, sir?" This from Sharon Szold, who had joined them at the blowup, to Sam White. "I'm a pilot also and might be of some help."

The director nodded; then David Szold said: "Are you sure you must go under the bridges?"

"We must." Bucher nodded. "And hugging the shore until we reach the two towers at the Plaza. And then what?" He looked at Sam White.

"Then we climb. Hard and fast. And keep climbing until we're at least six hundred feet—can he make it from six hundred feet, David? The Secretariat building is five hundred and fifty feet high. Only fifty feet isn't a lot of altitude to play around in."

"With the oversize sail, the craft has a six-to-one glide ratio. If you go as much as a hundred feet past the Secretariat building, Bucher, you'll crash headon into the south facade and plummet to earth like a stone."

Bucher grinned wryly. "Attaboy, David. That's the sort of encouragement I need." No less than half a dozen times since the building of the sky sail had started, David Szold had attempted to dissuade him from making the flight.

David Szold acknowledged the comment with a rather grim smile. "Also, we can't be certain that maneuvering device on the sail will function properly under flight conditions."

74

"It'll work." Bucher's tone was nothing if not confident; he winked largely at Sharon. "I have it straight from the front office that you're the best aerodynamics engineer in the business."

David shook his head in no little wonder and admiration. "If I were in your place, Bucher, I'm sure my attitude would at least be a little bit—somber."

"Now look . . ." Bucher made motions with his hands. "We'll be headed south in the plane and sail. If I cut the sail loose from the tow plane exactly at the south facade of the Secretariat building at six hundred feet altitude, which will give me exactly fifty feet to do it in, how many seconds will be required for me to bank right and land on the Secretariat's roof?"

"Well . . . with the sail directly above the shore line when you cut loose?"

"Right."

"Hmmmmmm . . . After climbing to six hundred feet you certainly won't have the same speed you had in passing under the bridges. . . . Four seconds, I'd say. Certainly not over six."

"Splendid, splendid. I want to be on top of the three bandits before they know what's up, before they kill that guard."

"I *still* think there must be another way." This from Sharon.

"There are several other ways," Bucher told her as White Hat's director motioned for one of the agents busy with packing the disassembled sky sail to answer the ringing phone at the opposite

75

end of the room. "But none with the surprise element of the sky sail. The bandits could spot a helicopter or parachutist long before they reached the Secretariat building, could shoot them down with ease, and of course the conventional glider is out. They land too fast. The Secretariat's roof is much too short for a conventional glider."

"But . . . perhaps if you tried hard you could get them to postpone their deadline until after dark, and then—"

"That wouldn't help a bit," David cut in. "Not the way the entire United Nations is lit up at night. Those atop the Secretariat building could see as clearly at night as during the day. Actually, waiting until nightfall would decrease Bucher's chance of success by close to fifty percent because he *must*, each second after passing under the bridges, keep his eyes open to prevent overshooting the mark, so to speak, and he would be going from the relative bright light of zero altitude to the darkness of six hundred feet altitude. His eyes simply would not have time to adjust to the lesser light; no person's eyes could manage it."

The White Hat agent who had answered the telephone now came to the group and whispered to the organization's director.

"But surely," Sharon insisted, "something could be done without all this risk to just one man. Something like using tear gas on the bandits and rushing them up the stairs and out the elevator shafts at the same time. Surely three bandits can't watch the stairs and eighteen elevator shafts. And with enough people mounting the assault they wouldn't have time to fling that poor guard over—"

"They already have, Sharon," Sam White said quietly.

All eyes focused on the aged, seamed face of White Hat's director.

"Say that again," Bucher said.

"That phone call a moment ago." The director's tone was heavy with a kind of despairing resignation. "It was from some of our people at the scene. At the Secretariat. A few minutes ago the three bandits threw the guard off the roof, then leaped to their deaths after him."

The long silence that followed was broken at last by Sharon Szold. "Well . . . if it had to be, better they than Bucher."

"But why the hell would the bandits kill themselves also?" Bucher asked no one in particular, thinking hard. "The guard, yes, but why suicide? And with hours remaining before their ultimatum deadline?"

The resignation was still in the director's voice. "It seems a student pilot was doing his first solo, freaked out when he discovered himself lost, and was headed straight for the UN at one thousand feet. The bandits apparently assumed the plane was after them, was coming to rescue the guard, so . . ."

"And the sky sail?" David Szold asked.

"I'll send it to the airport." The director grimaced sourly. "Someone will find a use for it one of these days." Then his tone lightened. "Or, we may give the sail a tryout, and if it performs as we'd hoped, I think we can find profitable use for the thing—providing you have no objection to our using your design, David."

"Not at all. You're welcome to it." David seemed pleased.

"With adequate compensation for using the design," Bucher put in with a meaningful glance at the director.

"Naturally," the director replied promptly. "Wouldn't have it any other way."

"Aw, come on," David Szold grinned, chiding. "The design is nothing revolutionary. It's not something any other aerodynamics engineer wouldn't have thought of under the same circumstances."

"Right." Bucher nodded, appreciating the other's philanthropy. "And any of hundreds of trained athletes can also make the hundred-yard dash with ease. But only one crosses the finish line first and he's the athlete who gets the purse. I'd say you've just crossed the line with your unique and radical sky sail design, David, so don't let another collect your prize."

Sharon drove Bucher back to his rented Oldsmobile parked near Bozeman's Bar. The incident with Tony Pelegroso had been explained to White Hat's director, so the police were not likely to hassle Boze Curdi over all the trouble at his place within the past twenty-four hours. Bucher was taking his leave of Sharon Szold and her little green Volks when, unaccountably, he abruptly recalled something Ali Annaser had told him earlier in the day, thinking he was Tony Pelegroso. He, as Pelegroso, had asked the Wog where he could find the Butcher, and the Wog had replied:

"I'm not sure. Ahmed Fowzie's people lost him last night in the vicinity of the Carlton Hotel; he's not registered at the Carlyle. That's certain. We've checked."

"What is it, Bucher?" Sharon's tone betrayed a tinge of urgency. He was leaving the Volks when she asked this.

"What is what?"

"I . . . for a second I thought I saw alarm on your face. But men of your mettle don't get alarmed, do they?"

"I've still got the phone numbers you gave me," he grinned. "If I find myself in need of a quick psychoanalysis I'll buzz you. Okay?"

She laughed softly, her rich contralto sending prickles over his flesh. "That is, without doubt, the very crudest brushoff I've ever been given. Why?"

"Later. Now scoot. And thank Rabbi Shimesh for sending you to protect me; I can handle myself from here on in." He wanted, suddenly, to get her away from this neighborhood as quickly as possible. If Ahmed Fowzie's men had been here last night, they were likely here today as well, and he saw no sense in placing the girl in jeopardy.

79

Bucher kept his eyes on the little bug until it became lost among the traffic in the distance. Only when he could no longer see the vehicle did he back away from the curb and, quite unintentionally, headed for Bozeman's Bar. So busy were his thoughts with weightier matters that he reached the bar's front door before realizing he was not headed in the direction of the rented Oldsmobile, which sat parked on the opposite side of the street a block away. Actually, the maroon vehicle sat in the next block, between what Bucher judged to be deserted tenement houses that lined both sides of the street the entire length of the block. The Olds was clearly visible from the front of Bozeman's Bar, where Bucher spun about in annoyance at his absent-minded oversight and glanced in the direction of his destination, to see a furtive figure scurrying away from the car in the opposite direction. Even so, an ordinary person would not have noticed anything suspicious—but ordinary people do not have "dead only" rewards of two hundred and fifty thousand dollars hanging over their heads.

Nevertheless, to anyone watching at the moment, and Bucher was abruptly of the opinion that there was not one but several people watching his every move, he gave no indication whatsoever to betray his opinion, but strode purposefully, even jauntily, up the street until he was opposite the Olds, then crossed over. Had the car been of a color lighter than maroon, he would have seen the greasy handprint on the hood sooner; as it was, he was halfway across the street before he saw it. It was near the front of the hood, as if some thoughtless mechanic with greasy hands had shoved the hood down to lock it in place. It told Bucher all he needed to know.

At the door of the vehicle he made a showy pretense of searching himself for the keys, of finding them and tossing them into the front seat, then began the only slightly altered routine of searching his pockets for cigarettes and finding none. As one in the final throes of a nicotine fit, he whirled angrily and stomped back toward Bozeman's Bar. And as he entered the joint, there popped up among his thoughts a memory from years ago in the Syndicate, the memory of a man with a slightly crippled right leg, whose name was Leo Natoni, called Bang-Bang Natoni throughout the underworld because of his expertise with high explosives—especially in booby-trapping automobiles. Moreover, the furtive figure he had seen scurrying away from the Olds moments ago had done so favoring his right leg; a snarl of the born predator washed over Bucher's hard face.

Not only were Ahmed Fowzie's creeps after him, but now the Syndicate was also bidding for a real blood-gutsy showdown. Surprisingly, the knowledge brought with it a kind of relief. He was getting absolutely nowhere fast in trying to locate Ahmed Fowzie, but he didn't have to look twice to know the identity of the person here in New York who'd given the go-ahead on him. This he already knew! Lupo "the Tiger" Sinetto! Less

81

than six months ago Sinetto had inherited the reins of command over the New York underworld —and with Lupo Sinetto Bucher knew how to deal.

Cautiously Bucher cracked the front door of Bozeman's Bar a fraction and peered out—and again the snarl of the predator washed over his hard face. Since he had entered the bar, the street outside, or rather the sidewalks, had grown uncommonly busy. Heretofore each time he had come to Bozeman's Bar there had been no pedestrians. Now, quite miraculously, there were four, all less than twenty-five yards from the bar's entrance where he stood and headed in his direction, each wearing the black leather jacket with white sleeves that he had recently learned from Sharon Szold was the sometimes local emblem of the Al Fat'ha. A fierce jolt of exultation streaked through Bucher's big frame. At last! Action at last! Action from the Al Fat'ha was something he could get his teeth into!

Bozeman Curdi, who had been on the phone when Bucher entered, watched with wide, fear-filled eyes as Bucher spun away from the front door and headed for the rear. Passing Curdi, Bucher tossed a hundred-dollar bill on the bar.

"Get on the horn and spread the word the Butcher is coming to see Lupo Sinetto, either with his invitation or without it."

Curdi started violently, bleating: "The Tiger?"

"Right," Bucher flung over his shoulder. "I'll check with you later to learn his address."

Bozeman Curdi neighed gently in unrefined terror at this.

Swiftly, silently, Bucher stepped through the rear door and swung powerfully, his brass-knucks-armored right fist crunching viciously into the Arabian features of the hulking crud sent to guard the bar's rear door. The man made only animal sounds of pain and distress as he collapsed, shattered face clutched in both hands.

"Mark one!" Bucher chuckled, knowing Ali Annaser now knew of his error in earlier assuming Bucher to be Tony Pelegroso. "So these bastards after me now won't settle for anything less than blood. Fifteen thousand dollars' worth of blood. Otherwise the Wog loses face and his own people shish kebab his fat ass." He glanced at the mutt he'd slugged with the knucks; the man would be eating soup for a long time to come. Bucher breathed deeply, feeling very good, casing the alley in which he stood. It ran the length of the block, was interrupted by cross streets at each end of the block, then continued its grubby, foul-smelling way through additional blocks in both directions—and it was just such a place as this that the approaching Al Fat'ha would consider ideal to trap him in. Which suited Bucher to a T. He was curious to learn just how smart and tough these Arab-Americans, his beloved fellow citizens, were, the bastards.

Moving swiftly and as silently as a shadow, Bucher went to the right, for down the alley some twenty yards from the bar's rear door a fire inspector's ladder led up to the roof. He mounted the ladder with the ease of a mountain cat and had just reached the roof three stories above when the four Al Fat'ha men he'd seen out front burst through the bar's rear entrance into the alley. Bucher listened.

"Balls of the Prophet!" exclaimed one in the American-Arabic dialect, which had a distinct accent of its own. "He clubbed Gamal with a baseball bat! Where did he go, Gamal, old buddy? Tell us where he went and we'll skin him alive with dull knives. Tell us. . . . Eh?" Silence. Then, in gleeful chortling: "We've *got* him, fellows! He's up on the roof! All we have to do is smoke him out, then close in! And take him alive if you can. I meant what I promised Gamal about skinning him with dull knives!"

In the following brief pause Bucher cleared his throat loudly and with great deliberation—might as well make it easy for the punks and get this hassle over with. He had a conference, of some sort, with Lupo "the Tiger" Sinetto, which he considered much more important than this. Already it was obvious to Bucher, who had graduated in back-alley, bloody warfare in Chicago years ago, that these cruds after him had a good deal to learn about such warfare. This conviction was strengthened enormously when he peeped over the edge of the roof seconds later and saw all four of his pursuers ascending, one after the other, the same metal ladder he himself had climbed. He shook his head in no little amazement; this would be like shooting fish in a barrel!

In one swift move he plucked the switchblade from its sheath at his left ankle, pressed the release, and watched the seven-and-a-half-inch sliver of steel flick into view and lock in place. Then he waited. Patiently. In silence. Until the first of the four climbing the ladder, the one who had done the talking below, reached the top of the ladder and was about to climb out onto the roof. At sight of Bucher crouched there, switchblade ready, his mouth flew wide to cry a warning, but the sound stuck in his throat as Bucher's blade darted forward, twice, like the darting tongue of a snake. At the needle-pointed pain in each wrist followed by the hot gush of his life's blood down each forearm, the cry suspended in his throat came violently unstuck in the form of one long, horrendous, gut-wrenching blast of sound. Bucher, ready and waiting when the blast subsided, thrust his face close to the other's and snarled quietly in the ancient Semitic dialect still found today on the Arabian Peninzula:

"I am the Evil Djinn sent by the enemies of thy ancestors to work a deadly curse on thee and thine, offal of the swine."

The man's dark face, round like a Holland cheese and hideously pock-marked, blanched the hue of aged dough, and a vulgar, fluttery farting sound escaped him; he let go of the top rung of the ladder, eyes rolling upward in their sockets.

Only his companions below him prevented the man from falling to his death. But they managed, Bucher watching until they almost reached the alley again; then his attention was drawn to the street in front of Bozeman's Bar once more. Two Al Fat'ha stood on the sidewalk in front of it, obviously on guard to prevent their quarry from escaping through the front of the place. Bucher hesitated only a moment before cupping both hands around his mouth and shouting in the American-Arab dialect: "Quickly! Quickly! That maroon Oldsmobile parked across the street in the next block is the Butcher's car! Move it lest he use it to escape!" Then he ducked behind a large brick chimney and waited.

The diminishing sounds of feet pounding the pavement told him both guards out front had taken the bait and were racing to the Olds. The pounding ceased; it was followed immediately by a distant ejaculation of delight from one of the Al Fat'ha at the vehicle, which informed Bucher they had discovered the car's keys in the front seat. Pause. Silence. Then Bucher's waiting behind the brick chimney ended. The sharp crack preceding the shattered blast that splintered nearby windows and rocked the neighborhood with sound informed Bucher the bomber had used two types of explosives—insurance against "dudding out"—the initial and smaller charge serving as a trigger for the second and larger. Either charge was sufficient to kill anyone in the vehicle; the two together could smear any occupants like a bloody paste, beyond all hope of identification, over a city block.

On the heels of the explosion Bucher stood. The neighborhood was quiet as death except for the muted whine of an automobile engine racing at high speed, and as he peered over the edge of the roof he saw a long, black, curtained limousine careen around the corner and out of sight beyond the explosion area. A frown of perplexity washed across his hard features. Three times now he had seen the mysterious black limousine, assuming it had been the same vehicle each time, and he was beginning to suspect it was. The first time he'd seen it was at Rabbi Shimesh's home, the second at the 99 Names theater, and now here, which was too much to be mere coincidence. His frown of perplexity deepened. . . .

The three unscathed Al Fat'ha and their two wounded comrades were gone when Bucher descended and reentered Curdi's Crudhouse. As usual, Boze Curdi, in the cringing attitude of abject servility, stood behind the bar, this time with a slip of note paper in one hand. This he extended across the bar as Bucher entered.

"It's a phone number you're to call, Bucher," he quavered. "They said the Ti-Tiger wants to see you worser'n you want to see him."

"They who?"

"Fatso F-Fain and G-Gunboat Dru." Curdi's Adam's apple did nip-ups.

"Christ! Are they still around?" Fain and Dru

both were relics of the old days. "And what does Lupo Sinetto want to see me about?"

"They never said, Bucher, only that he was in a real lather to chew the fat with you. Sounded real friendly like. ... Er ... Bucher?"

"Yeah?" Bucher folded the note paper and thrust it into his shirt pocket.

"That big bang up the street . . . what was it, Bucher?"

"Couple of guys got blown to hell playing with dynamite. You seen Leo Natoni lately?"

Curdi thought hard for a moment. "Bang-Bang Natoni?"

"That's right."

"He's dead as far as I know. According to the grapevine. Two, maybe three years ago he took an outside contract offered by some underground rebel outfit to blow up a munitions works somewhere down in Georgia. A factory that produced high-explosives, that's what it was. Well, Bang-Bang blasted the factory all right, and himself too, along with twenty-five other people who worked there. Anyway, that's the story that got out. When the factory blew there wasn't enough left of the people there to bury. They buried empty coffins with names on 'em."

"And Natoni too?" The man had been one of the best high-explosive men Bucher had ever seen. But accidents did happen.

"And Natoni too, so far as I know, Bucher."

On impulse Bucher asked: "Where's Lorili these

days?" He spoke as if he knew the woman, though he'd never met her.

"Lorili?" Curdi shifted from foot to foot uneasily, his eyes doing the same in search of something to fix on. At last, as though with tremendous effort, he said: "Well—she's out on the West Coast sommers. Trying to make it big in the movies. And she will make it big, by God, once she gets a toehold—and I pity the poor bastard that gives it to her. Leastwise I heard she was out on the coast. I ain't seen her since . . . well . . . you know. I for damn sure ain't got nothing a dame like her'd want. Why you ask, Bucher?"

"Just a thought. I wouldn't know the woman if we bumped on the street." Bucher's part in this trivial discourse had become automatic, his mind busy with half a dozen different aspects of his current assignment: locating and rescuing the five kidnapped Israelis before all hell broke loose between Arabs and Jews in New York. And Lupo "the Tiger" Sinetto just might have some information on the matter—since there was damn little that took place in the city outside the law he didn't know about.

Police sirens were howling their way to the scene of his rented maroon Oldsmobile's explosion when Bucher left the bar. He walked in the opposite direction, away from the ugly crater where the Olds had been parked. Nothing of the vehicle was left, except for a few chunks of metal driven into the earth by the blast. The facade of the weary tenement house on that side of the street sagged in total ruin. One cockeyed thing was certain—the sonofabitch who'd boobytrapped the Olds wanted him dead in the worst way. But it hadn't been Leo Natoni.

Bucher called the number Curdi had given him at the drugstore of a small neighborhood shopping center several blocks from the bar. He at once recognized the gravelly voice of Gunboat Dru over the wire. The old mobster sounded positively overjoyed that he called.

During the early days of Prohibition, before big-city crime bosses organized to produce enough alcohol to appease the enormous thirst of the Roaring Twenties, each week thousands of gallons of Cuban rum poured into the East Coast. It was during this time that Dru earned the name "Gunboat." With a dozen World War I water-cooled .30-caliber machine guns and two obsolete English 3-pounder cannons, he converted a fast luxury yacht into a fast gunboat and announced to rumrunners one and all that he was offering protection from hijackers for their cargoes between Cuba and the United States. Soon all in the illegal rum transportation business were his clients, a circumstance Dru himself brought about by the simple and forthright expedient of sinking any cargo not under his protection—hence the name Gunboat. If the old geezer had another name, Bucher had never heard it. Dru was so overjoyed at Bucher's call, he was largely incoherent.

"Hold it, hold it!" Bucher finally managed to break in. "Slow down and say that again."

After several seconds of gaspy sounds of excited breathing, the gravelly voice resumed more slowly. "I said Tiger done passed out the word that them two hundred and fifty Gs on your noggin has been lifted whilst you're here in New York. That anybody what hits you has to reckon with his torpedoes; I mean the Tiger's torpedoes and that ain't hay, see."

"Why?" Bucher frowned, wondering. It was not like Lupo Sinetto to countermand an order from the top, although he was very near the top himself.

"Why?" Dru sounded flabbergasted.

"That's right, dammit. Why does Lupo suspend the dead-only hit price on my head while I'm in New York?"

"Well—uh—why, you smartassed young whippersnapper! If I had my way I'd take a belt to your—huh?"

Bucher could not restrain a grin as Gunboat talked to a third party on his end of the line. Then Lupo Sinetto's satiny smooth voice came over the wire.

"Butchy?"

"Yeah?"

"Can we meet somewhere?"

"And do what?"

"Talk. I got a proposition."

"For me? You nuts?"

"It'll put the amount of the hit price on your

head in your pocket. And Gunboat was straight about my suspending the reward on your head while you're in New York. We do this piece of business together and maybe I can get it cancelled for keeps. The thing—"

"Lupo?" Bucher interrupted quietly, although his pulse was gaining speed. With the hit price on his head cancelled for keeps, he and Kleyr could live in peace. "Lupo, if this is a setup to burn me, you better think twice."

Only when the other's near-hysterical pleading jumped at him from the phone did Bucher realize Lupo Sinetto had lost his cool, but good. The man was desperate, though for what reason Bucher was unable to determine. But he did hear the name Ahmed Fowzie several times. This in itself decided Bucher. He agreed to meet with Sinetto who, with Gunboat as chauffeur of the large Pontiac station wagon, would pick him up at the shopping center within half an hour.

They arrived in twenty minutes, the scrawny, ancient Gunboat Dru at the wheel, the equally ancient deaf mute Fatso Fain, no longer fat and because of it looked like a hundred-and-fifty-pound man in a three-hundred-pound skin, beside him in the front seat, while soft and pink and criminally brilliant Lupo "the Tiger" Sinetto sat in the rear, a valise resembling an oversize sample case in his lap. The special heavy-duty tires on the station wagon plus the solid, weighted sway of its action when Gunboat braked it to a halt at the shopping center led Bucher to suspect the Pontiac wore armor plate and bullet-proof glass. Which, under the circumstances, was not a bad idea at all. More than one mobster in New York would like to shoot Sinetto from the saddle and take his place.

"It's your show," Bucher told Sinetto without ceremony as he joined the man in back. Fain grinned in toothless salutation as Dru nodded vigorously. Lupo Sinetto gulped nervously but said nothing until the Pontiac was well away from the shopping center. Even then, for openers, he shoved the heavy valise over to Bucher with: "I upped it a quarter; there's half a million in unmarked bills there—Okay?"

"Okay for what?" Bucher growled, opening the valise and noting the neatly stacked packages of twenties and hundreds inside. "Who you want burned?"

"Ahmed Fowzie!" Sinetto's tone was the epitome of frustration and rage.

Bucher pretended to consider the matter, then nodded. "Fair enough. I'll make the hit. But where do I find the son of a bitch?"

"That's it!" the other almost screeched. "Ain't nobody can find Ahmed Fowzie! Don't nobody know where the bastard is holed up, if he's holed up; or where he hangs out, if he hangs out; where he eats, if he eats; where he screws, if he screws —ain't nobody knows nothing about the bastard! But he's gotta exist, ain't he, Bucher? He's tear-

ing my organization all to hell so he's gotta exist, ain't he?"

"How come he's tearing your organization all to hell?" Bucher asked, suddenly much more interested in this than in the half a million dollars in the valise.

"He's buying my key people right out from under my nose, that's how come," Sinetto said, getting a grip on himself. "He's local god of the anti-Jewish faction of the Arabs here in the city, the way I get it. But what the hell does he want with my people? That's what clobbers my balls. He ain't in the rackets. Wouldn't know what one was if he met it face to face on the sidewalk— you remember Johnny Ungo? The ace torpedo?"

Bucher nodded. He knew Johnny Ungo all right.

"Ahmed Fowzie hired him day before yesterday. Right out from under my nose he hired him."

"I thought Johnny was freelance," Bucher said.

"He was, dammit. But we had an understanding, you might say. Johnny was supposed to freelance for me. But that damn A-rab Fowzie made him an offer of half a million a year, *plus* a fee for any jobs Johnny pulled. Half a million a year as retainer for a torpedo! There ain't a man in the business who'd turn it down."

"Why does Fowzie hire a torpedo of Johnny's caliber, then send to Chicago for a bum like Tony Pelegroso?" Bucher wondered aloud.

"Huh?"

Bucher explained briefly about his hassle with

Pelegroso and the Al Fat'ha, whereupon the other nodded understandingly.

"That clears up something I been hearing," Sinetto volunteered. "The grapevine said a big torpedo was coming from Chi to do a big job, which would be Pelegroso and you, Bucher, but Johnny is to burn the winner either way, so I guess that means you again."

"Johnny Ungo is to make a bid for me?"

"You sound like you don't believe it."

"Oh, I believe it all right; Johnny'd burn his mother for a two-dollar bill. I just thought Johnny might have more sense than to—" Instinctively Bucher whipped around to stare out the rear window. The large black limousine bore down on the station wagon like a runaway express—and the ugly snout of the tommygun peeking through the rear window was not a friendly greeting card.

"*Down!*" Bucher seized Lupo Sinetto by the nape and hurled him bodily to the floorboards as the mindless yammer of the limousine's tommygun played a deadly tattoo over the rear side windows of the Pontiac. The stuttery squeal of tires followed as the limousine streaked forward and out of sight around a corner; Gunboat Dru fought the wheel and ground the station wagon to a halt. It was over almost before it began, as Bucher and Lupo Sinetto returned to their seats. But it was a thoroughly shattered Lupo Sinetto; his face had the pallor of an untended corpse and his pudgy hands shook; the fear of death was

95

with him like a physical presence. It pinched his eyes and shrunk his cheeks and drew a puckered line around his mouth. Three or four times he strove to articulate, only to hiccough violently, at last managing lamely: "T-T-Thanks, Bucher."

Bucher shook his head grimly. "No thanks necessary." His cold eyes traced the ragged row of dots on the bullet-proof glass of the raised windows. "But if this Pontiac wasn't armored it'd be another story. Gunboat—Fatso. Did either of you eyeball the trigger man?"

"I never," Gunboat Dru growled. "But—wait!" He concentrated on frantic motions the deaf mute Fatso Fain was making with both hands. Then, in amazement: "God almighty." He turned to gape toward Bucher and his boss. "Fats here says the man behind the chopper was Johnny Ungo!"

"Fatso, are you sure?" Bucher leaned forward as he spoke, studying the face of the other, touching his shoulder to get his attention, then repeating the question slowly, so Fain could read his lips. Fain's reply was a vigorous yes.

"I knew it, I knew it," Lupo Sinetto wailed, hysteria edging his tone. "Ahmed Fowzie is aiming to take over the rackets in New York and he's beginning with me and my operations!"

Bucher said nothing, but he knew the other was wrong. The attempted hit had not been directed at Lupo Sinetto, but at him. "I'd give a pretty penny to know who owns that limousine," Bucher said grimly.

Gunboat Dru had lined the Pontiac station wagon

out again, but now pulled to the side of the street, ancient eyes on the man beside him in the front seat. After fumbling about in the dash compartment a moment, he scribbled a number on a slip of paper and handed it to Bucher. "Fatso says that's the license number of the limousine. It was coated with grease so's to pick up lots of dust and the like, but if Fatso says that's the number, that's the number. He's good at things like that."

Bucher took the number and glanced questioningly at Sinetto, who nodded, saying: "Gunboat's right. If Fatso says that's the number then that's it." He leaned toward Bucher, in better control of himself now and speaking confidentially. "Are you going to handle this yourself, Bucher?"

"Providing we can make a deal."

"But there's half a million in that valise. Count it—"

"Damn the half million," Bucher said flatly. "I'm more interested in that quarter of a million dead-only reward the Syndicate's got on my head. I want it cancelled permanently. For keeps. You got that much suction with Mr. Big?"

Lupo "the Tiger" Sinetto tried to match Bucher's cold, hard gaze with a crafty stare and failed miserably.

"I don't know if I can swing it or not, Butchy," he finally mumbled thickly, self-consciously, eyes lowered. "There's some things Mr. Big is stubborn as hell about."

"Okay, punk," Bucher snarled softly. "Either you get it lifted or you finger Mr. Big for me, personally. Refuse and I come looking for you. How's that for a deal?" In a quick aside: "Hold it, Gunboat. I'm getting out here."

All color vanished from Sinetto's puffy countenance. "You mean you'll burn Mr. Big?" The question reeked of incredulity. "You mean— *actually?*"

"Do we deal?" Bucher's eyes were ruthless, uncompromising.

Sinetto nodded a bit dumbly at first, then violently. "Yeah, Bucher. We deal. I'll do my best to get the hit price on your head cancelled, and if anybody can do it, I can."

"When you succeed, phone the info in to this number." Bucher, having memorized the license number of the black limousine, wrote the same White hat blind number he'd left with Ali Annaser on the slip of paper Dru had given him and handed it to Sinetto. "Okay?"

"Yeah, Bucher. Yeah! Okay . . . whatever you say. Uh—take the valise. It's yours."

"Huh-uh." Bucher opened the door on his side. "I'm donating it to your funeral fund in case you fail. If I don't hear something over that number I gave you within twelve hours, I'm going on a tiger hunt. Understand?"

"Yeah, Bucher." Sinetto was mumbling again, eyes on his feet. "I understand."

"Good." Bucher's grin projected rakehell camaraderie. "I wouldn't want a misunderstanding to louse up an old friendship like ours." He dismounted from the Pontiac as Sinetto responded with a hint of hysteria.

"Hey! Hey!-yeah-Hey! Hey! An old friendship like ours, hey!-hey!"

6

After leaving Sinetto and company it took
Bucher exactly ten minutes on the phone contact-
ing old acquaintances of his Syndicate days to
learn that Johnny Ungo's favorite hangout was
a West Side dollhouse called the Pink Pussycat.
He took a cab.

"And don't push it," he told the cabby. He
needed time to think and perhaps adopt a new
tack. He sure as hell was getting nowhere fast in
locating the five kidnapped Israelis on his present
course. Damn! He'd also meant to call Kleyr.
With nothing to do but watch television she'd be
climbing the walls before long. What was it
Sharon Szold had said about Kleyr? "Everybody
knows Kleyr. Everybody in the New York Jewish
community." Yeah, that was it. Perhaps he should

return to the apartment at the Carlyle, acquaint Kleyr with the situation as he understood it thus far—or misunderstood it—and let her put her high-powered, sixteen-cylinder, genius-caliber intellect to work seeking a solution.

"But first I want a crack at that goddamn Johnny Ungo," Bucher growled to himself—because something was as queer as all getout with Ungo's tommygun try from the black limousine. As recently as yesterday Ungo had been in Lupo Sinetto's employ; therefore, *Ungo had known Sinetto's Pontiac station wagon was bullet-proof.* So why the try with the tommygun? In public? In broad open daylight? And Bucher had little doubt the try was for him and not for Lupo Sinetto. And what in the holy hell was with that black limousine? The damn thing was becoming his nemesis, for he had a feeling that, except for the first time he'd seen it—outside Rabbi Shimesh's home—it was always the same vehicle. There were two identical limousines, of this he was positive, for the license-plate number of the vehicle Gunboat Dru had given him was entirely different from the license plate number of the limousine in which he had seen Maud Ann Beeker cruise past Rabbi Shimesh's home. Anyway, what would Maud Ann Beeker need top gunsels such as Johnny Ungo for? Perhaps he would learn some answers at the Pink Pussycat.

The Pink Pussycat greeted Bucher's entrance into its dimly lit confines with that redolent mélange common to the cocktail bar-cum-bordello the world over, and he at once identified Ungo's reason for favoring it as a hangout: the girls were young, they were lovely, and they were top- and bottomless. He chose a booth that allowed him to see both the front and rear of the long, low room and that put a solid wall at his back. A bare young thing wearing a lustful pout slid into the booth beside him—and yelped shrilly in alarm as she gathered herself off the floor across the room.

"Okay, wise guy! Out!-Out!-Out!" The bouncer materialized out of nowhere—thick-shouldered, long-armed, with a labored, apelike waddle to his powerful body, snarling at Bucher. "Hit the side-walk, bum, else I throw you through a wall—"

"Crack!"

Bucher's backhand, with all his weight behind it, spun the bouncer completely around and—

"Crack!"

—a second backhand met him, spun him back, whereupon his painful revolutions ceased with an ugly crunch when the edge of Bucher's hand axed him brutally across the bridge of the nose. Tears streaming from his eyes, blood and mucus streaming from his mouth and nose, the bouncer screamed like a dozen wild banshees stoned on Bushmill's best and pawed his way, literally, out of the room, stumbling over tables, chairs, several young bawds who had appeared, and all else in his path to a door in the rear.

"Gee, mister," said the girl Bucher had thrown bodily from his booth. "You better leave while

102

you can. Elmer—the bouncer—he's good with a knife. If I were you I'd go—please?"

Bucher resumed his seat and studied her for a moment. Her lustful pout was gone and she looked somewhat frazzled about the edges, a look Bucher knew all too well—the look of a young woman who was weary of fighting the wolf with pennies and had begun hustling to make ends meet. Chances were a hundred to one she had dependents at home. He flipped a fifty-dollar bill on the table in front of him and motioned for her to sit down.

"You won't throw me out again?" she asked hesitantly, taking a seat nonetheless.

"No. Not again," he lied boldly. "I wouldn't have thrown you out the first time except I wanted a crack at Elmer." He indicated the fifty between them. "Take it. It's yours. Buy the kid a pair of shoes."

Her eyes grew large. "How did you know? Only it's twins. Both girls. I—" She ceased abruptly, casting a furtive glance over her shoulder. "We're not supposed to discuss our personal lives with the customers," she whispered. "Let's talk about something else, huh?"

"What's your name? Not your house name. Your real name."

"Why?"

"Because I'm your uncle come all the way from Virginia to see his favorite niece, so I'd best know your name."

"May Green. That's my real name. My house

103

name is Prissy." She squinted quizzically. "But why the game, mister?"

Bucher gave her another fifty. "We can't let one of the twins go barefoot, can we? Game? I'm waiting on someone. And while we're waiting, one game is good as another." He caught the flicker of fear that washed across her face a second before she asked:

"Now what's your name, mister?"

"My friends call me Bucher."

The low moan of terror came from somewhere deep down in her naked body and her young-old, weary face blanched the unwholesome color of white-flour dough too long exposed to the air.

"The Butcher?" The whispered words were more an accusation than a question. "You're *the Butcher?"* She struggled to stand and move away from him but seemed for the moment to have lost the use of her legs.

"Where's Johnny Ungo?" Bucher asked quietly, holding her eyes with his. She shivered suddenly, as one freezing.

"D-Don't *look* at me l-like *that!* God—have *mercy!"*

"Earn that hundred dollars, woman," he said, still quietly. "Where's Johnny Ungo?"

She spoke through stiff, awkward lips. "They'll kill me when they learn I've been talking to the Butcher."

"They who?"

"Johnny and—and somebody named Ahmed Fowzie he talks to on the phone."

104

"When does Fowzie come here?"

"Never, that I know of. He only phones."

Bucher nodded, already suspecting as much. "And Ungo?"

"He's supposed to be out—looking for you. For the Butcher."

"Okay, beat it. You've earned the hundred." For the benefit of those watching and possibly for the safety of May Green, Bucher drew one hand back as if to strike her and spat savagely: "Get the hell away from me, you damn tramp! And stay away!" Nor did he miss the look of gratitude in the girl's eyes as she found the use of her legs and sprang from the booth like a wild thing, rushing off, motioning some of the onlooking bawds to follow her as she did so. The door behind which Elmer, the bouncer, had disappeared opened as she neared it, the hulking Elmer outlined in the light from a hall behind him, a huge knife in his bloody fist. He started toward Bucher as May Green passed, whispering: "Elmer! He's *the Butcher!*" whereupon Elmer stopped as one stunned with a pole axe, the knife dropping from his hand unnoticed, as he turned and hurried after May Green and the girls following her.

Bucher scanned the barroom with cold eyes. Except for a seedy-looking barkeep with him, pomaded hair and a black rubber bow tie, he had the place to himself. Though only for a minute. Then Johnny Ungo came through the front door. The dapper, dissipated-handsome Ungo froze in his tracks when he saw the ugly, thick-barreled, silencered Walther P–38 in Bucher's hand, aimed at his heart. Bucher snarled softly:

"Make with the words, you son of a bitch. The right words, punk, else I spatter your stupid brains all over the wall behind you."

Some seconds passed before Ungo won the struggle to recover from the shock of seeing his nightmare of being under the Bucher's gun, which often disturbed his sleep, become a raw reality.

"Ha, ha," he ventured timidly. "Aw, hell now, Butchy—"

"Koosh!"

The Walther in Bucher's hand sighed gently— and Johnny Ungo lurched sideways, clawing at his creased hip where the 9mm slug had cut the belt supporting his trousers.

"You used the wrong words, son of a bitch," Bucher told the man politely. "Use 'em again and I give you a nine-millimeter belly button an inch or two below the one Mother Nature gave you. Okay?"

Ungo gaped, clutching his trousers. He'd been in some tight spots in his life, but he had never been closer to death than he was at this moment and he knew it. Without considering the consequences of his vacillation he decided then and there to do whatever was necessary to survive this encounter with the dread Butcher.

"Wh-what words you wanna hear, Butchy?" He swallowed noisily—a rusty sound.

"First about the black limousine. Who drove it?"

"They's a curtain between the back and the driver. A heavy curtain. And I was ordered not to try to look at who drove. Only talk."

"And you obeyed?"

The other nodded, hitching his trousers tighter.

"But you knew Sinetto's Pontiac was bullet-proof, didn't you?" Bucher continued.

Ungo nodded, gulping again, bowels feeling loose from a massive onslaught of relief; at least there was this one thing in his favor. He nodded brightly.

"'Course I knew it. I've been driving it for Lupo until a couple of days ago."

"Then why make your play for me when I'm in a bullet-proof car?"

"Because I was told to," Ungo said doggedly. "And that's the truth."

"Who told you?"

"The guy I work for. Ahmed Fowzie."

"And you never told him the Pontiac was bullet-proof."

"He never asked me. Just called me on the phone, told me where the limousine'd be waiting, and instructed me what to do. That's all. Then he hung up. There wasn't no time to tell him nothing. There never is. He always says what he's got to say, then hangs up and that's it."

"And that's the way he hired you away from Sinetto?"

"Yeah. He told me where a half million dollars was in escrow, waiting to be placed in my name if I went to work for him—hell, Bucher, I can't

107

turn down geetus like that. Half a million. And that's only a retainer. To keep me on call, sort of. Yeah, it was all arranged by phone. I ain't never laid eyes on the guy in person. Wouldn't know him from Adam's off ox."

"But you're supposed to burn me for having put Tony Pelegroso on ice—right?" An image was beginning to emerge in Bucher's mind, the image of a man with a blank face. As Pelegroso had said at Boze Curdi's bar, "Ain't nobody never seen Ahmed Fowzie." It was beginning to appear to Bucher as if Pelegroso had known exactly what he'd been talking about. But why all the mystery?

Ungo took a deep breath; it was true he had orders from Fowzie to gun the survivor of the Bucher-Pelegroso hassle, and since the man with a gun on him now also knew it, he saw little point in denial.

"Yeah. That's right, Bucher. Fowzie's orders were to burn the survivor of your hassle with Pelegroso."

Without removing his bleak eyes from the man, Bucher leathered his piece. "Okay, Johnny. You pack a heater under your arm, a 32–20 as I recall. Let's get the show on the road."

Johnny Ungo stared, hardly daring to believe his eyes and ears. Somewhere, though, he'd heard the Butcher was going soft and had refused to believe it. But he no longer refused to believe. It was *true!* A thrill of exultation shot through him. Never in his life had he doubted his speed and ability with the 32–20 in his shoulder rig and he did not doubt now. He knew beyond question he could take the Butcher if given an even chance, which he was being given right now—

Ungo's revolver appeared to leap into his hand like a thing alive and he snapped it on—

"Koosh!-Koosh!-Koosh!"

The triple sigh of the Walther in Bucher's big mitt sledgehammered death through Johnny Ungo's head, and he died without pulling the trigger or knowing what killed him, as the three 9mm slugs wrenched him off the floor and hurled him backward toward the front entrance of the Pink Pussycat.

"Just too damn dumb to stay alive," Bucher muttered to himself, snapping a fresh clip into the Walther and returning the gun to its holster. "Too damn egotistic to turn his back and walk away." He turned to speak to the bartender, only to discover that he and the man he'd just killed were the only ones remaining in the place. Down at the far end of the bar a pay phone pealed shrilly, demanding attention. Once, twice, thrice its irritating stridency raked over Bucher's nerves; on the fifth ring he got it and grunted into the receiver. A hollow, sepulchral voice, as though speaking from deep in a tomb, said:

"Mr. Johnny Ungo, please. Tell him Ahmed Fowzie is calling."

Bucher frowned, thinking hard. He'd never heard a human voice sound like Fowzie's did. "Johnny can't come to the phone." He hadn't really intended to say it. It just came out like that. If he could keep this bum talking—

The voice grew stern, authoritative, but still as if spoken from a tomb. "Tell him Ahmed Fowzie is calling."

Yet there was no point in keeping the bum talking, Bucher reasoned, for there was nothing he could do about discerning Fowzie's identity over the phone like this.

"No can do," he replied jovially, though not feeling jovial. "Johnny won't listen."

The voice from the tomb was haughtily contemptuous, icy. "And why not?"

"I just killed the sonofabitch, that's why not."

Silence. Stone-cold, solid silence. Then: "Wh-who're you?"

"The Butcher, you bastard, and you're next on my list. I gut-shoot you on sight."

Fowzie slammed down the phone so hard Bucher was forced to biff his temple gently several times with the heel of his hand to stop the ringing in his ear. He grinned sourly. Ahmed Fowzie was a sociable cuss, wasn't he. Real friendly like.

Bucher fished a dime from his pocket and fed Ma Bell's little public monster, then dialed White Hat.

"This is the Iceman."

"Just a moment."

Some seconds passed before White Hat's director came on the wire and identified himself. Again he and Bucher conversed in the long-dead Serbo-Croatian dialect. In as few words as possible,

110

Bucher gave him a rundown of what had happened since their last meeting, concluding with the destruction of his rented Oldsmobile and requesting that White Hat dig up any information available on one Leo Natoni, known throughout the underworld as Bang-Bang Natoni.

"The medics have uncovered a weirdo with the three Al Fat'ha who jumped off the Secretariat building at the United Nations," the director said when Bucher finished. "Each of them had enough LSD-3 and hashish in his system to clobber an ox."

"What's LSD-3?" Bucher asked. Obviously it was some sort of drug, though he'd never heard of it before.

"We're not sure yet. Army has been experimenting with it on twenty-five hundred volunteers, hoping to find some use for it in warfare. One strong hypothesis says it alters personality to what is called a yes-and-no perspective."

"You mean all black or all white? No gray areas?"

"That's it. No gray areas at all."

"Jesus! Then the three Al Fat'ha on the Secretariat had no intention of waiting for the plans of Nabil Chehade Shazar's hydrogen motor to be delivered to them."

"That's exactly the way I've got it figured, but the presence of hashish in their systems puzzle me. LSD-3 has neither taste nor odor, and a tiny pinpoint drop is all it takes—"

"And Arabs usually don't smoke hash," Bucher

111

put in. "They take it with strong black tea. Therefore, the three Arabs on the Secretariat could
have been given the LSD-3 either in the tea or the
hash, or both, without their knowing it. Right?"

"Right."

"But to what end?" Bucher realized the answer
to his question even as he asked it.

"Because anybody under its influence can be
talked into doing virtually anything. If the three
dead Al Fat'ha had unknowingly taken LSD-3,
I'd say they did so shortly before going to the
Secretariat building; they probably took hash to
bolster their courage and the LSD-3 was in it.
Then, when the LSD-3 took effect, their entire
view of their situation altered drastically. The
black-and-white personality. They knew they were
right but saw their situation as utterly hopeless,
which left them no choice at all but to do what
they did."

"Yeah." This was Bucher's only comment; his
thoughts were racing a mile a minute. If Ahmed
Fowzie had a supply of LSD-3, triggering a kill-
quick-or-die hassle between the Al Fat'ha and the
Jewish Defense League would be no problem at
all. What's more, he could trigger it without anyone being aware it was he who did it. "See what
our technicians can come up with on that peculiar
sound to Fowzie's voice. I've got to find that punk,
but quick."

"Do you know a Mrs. Charles Latham Billingsley? She wants to see you. She contacted the local
police, asking your whereabouts, and the police

112

contacted the local FBI, who contacted Washington. I took the call from there. She claims your Aunt Maude Ann has been gravely injured in an auto accident and left her address. I didn't know you had an Aunt Maude Ann."

"Neither did I until right now. What's the address?" Bucher listened attentively as the director gave him the address, the slight frown on his face growing darker when the other finished. "That's Rockefeller Center," he growled testily.

"I know. I wanted to see if you'd catch it. You're to meet her on the eastern side of the plaza; there is a flower-lined walk New Yorkers have dubbed the "English Channel" due to the British- and French-leased buildings flanking it on either side. She'll be waiting near the first fountain from Fifth Avenue; it smacks of a setup to me. But there's no need of my suggesting that you exercise extreme caution. You want me to send some help along?"

"No. This has nothing to do with the Israeli-Arab hassle." He explained about seeing Maude Ann Beeker cruise past Rabbi Shimesh's home early that morning in a curtained limousine. "My guess is that Mrs. Charles Latham Billingsley and Maud Ann Beeker are one and the same person. Maude Ann once worked for me as a doxy in North Carolina. She's probably scored big on the marriage market and, since seeing me this morning, fears I might upset her matrimonial apple cart in some way, and wants my assurance that I'll say nothing. Okay, I'm going past Rockefeller

113

Plaza anyway. I'll stop by and see what's galling her. Incidentally, Kleyr has resigned from the organization."

"Is that so?" The director sounded surprised. "She hasn't told me."

"I'm telling you. It's official as of last night. She's no longer a member of this rat race."

"I won't deny that White Hat could use her genius to tremendous advantage, but I'm really glad she's out. I figured that's the way it'd be whenever you learned of it." There was honest relief in the older man's voice. "She'll—" Silence. Then: "Hang on—it's the latest results on our other efforts to locate the five kidnapped members of Israel's United Nations mission." Again silence, during which Bucher puzzled absently at Johnny Ungo's courage to brace him in a showdown. Movement also at the rear of the dimly lit room caught his attention; May Green stood in the doorway. She now wore a simple print frock with lace collar. Bucher motioned for her to draw near as White Hat's director came back on the wire.

"Nothing new," he said tonelessly. "But a headless body which otherwise fits the description of one of the kidnapped Israelis, Jacob Radak, has been found in the East River. And within spitting distance, you might say, of the United Nations. Cripes, if the fingerprints turn out to be Radak's and word of his death leaks to the press, we'll have dozens of dead Arabs on our hands by sundown—the Jewish Defense League'll run amok."

"No ransom demands from the kidnappers yet?"

"Not yet—wait!" Bucher could hear the director talking to someone, then: "Yes. There's been a ransom demand—*damn!* It's the same demand made by the three Al Fat'ha members who flung the security guard off the top of the Secretariat building and jumped after him."

"The original plans of Nabil Chehade Shazar's hydrogen motor? Hell, neither the Israelis nor the U.S. will pay those as ransom. Money, yes, even gold bullion, but not Shazar's hydrogen motor. Not for a thousand kidnapped victims. They'd be crazy to. See what you can dig up on Bang-bang Natoni. I'll check back later."

"Yes?" May Green asked, stopping in front of him as Bucher hung up the phone. He pointed toward the dead Johnny Ungo. "Friend of yours?"

She did not look toward the dead man and spoke through clenched teeth. "I hated his guts! I've seen some freaky heads in my time, but he took the cake."

"A head? Narcotics?" The underworld grapevine had never mentioned Ungo as an addict, which meant nothing.

"Well—yes, narcotics and something else too. Hash, for one thing. Hash was his favorite, but on occasion he took something that made an altogether different person out of him. And when he got that way nobody could reason with him or change his mind about anything he had his head set on."

"Who was his supplier?. For the hash?" The young woman's description of the drug Ungo had

115

taken in addition to hash tallied with the effects of LSD-3. "Ahmed Fowzie?"

"I don't know for sure," May Green said. "I mean, I ain't seen Ahmed Fowzie actually hand Johnny any narcotics, but usually when Johnny had one of his queer spells it'd be soon after he'd talked with Fowzie."

"Johnny told me he'd never seen Fowzie."

"Yes." She nodded vigorously. "That's my understanding also. But several times after talking to Fowzie he'd leave, then return shortly with a small package that looked like it'd been sent through the mails; there's a post office a few blocks west of here."

"I see." Bucher's cold gaze swept across the man he'd recently killed as he turned toward the door, saying over his shoulder: "Better warn the other girls to get their clothes on. This place'll be crawling with cops in a little while."

Several times, even before the shootout with Johnny Ungo, Bucher's ears had detected that frying sound that comes over a radio receiver when there is no other signal on it. When there is a signal the sound is called static, but without another signal it is best described as a frying sound. And now, as Bucher was about to exit the Pink Pussycat, as he passed the body of Johnny Ungo, this frying sound became much more pronounced. He was stepping over an outflung arm when there was an abrupt silencing of the sound, and from the corpse of the man he had killed came the words: "Haw! Haw! Haw! I guess that's

116

one speed trap the cops'll have to vacate!" Bucher stopped, almost in midstride, and stared down at the corpse at his feet. His concept of reality forbade assuming a superstition such as a dead man talking, yet he was understandably curious as to the manner in which the words were produced, suspecting all the while that he already knew. Nor was he incorrect, Bucher noted with satisfaction when he knelt beside the corpse. Slung over Ungo's shoulder by a leather strap, and worn under his coat, was one of those small citizen band radio transceivers becoming so popular of late. Moreover, it was one of the expensive models. Bucher unbuckled the thing, pulled it free of its previous owner, and continued on out of the Pink Pussycat. Bucher had little hope of the transceiver leading to any new information regarding the kidnapped Israelis, but he was in a position at the moment in which he could take no chances, overlook no clue, however unimportant it might seem at the moment.

7

On the eastern side of Rockfeller Plaza, at the
flower-lined walk dubbed the English Channel,
near the first fountain from Fifth Avenue, Bucher
found Maud Ann Beeker, now Mrs. Charles Latham Billingsley. She was seated on one of the
small park benches, and about her was none of
the hard-nosed, merciless greed and determination to claw her way to the top at all costs that
had been so obvious when he had known her years
ago. In fact, to judge by her appearance, Maud
Ann was already at the top, for her clothes were
the best money could buy from shops in New York
and Paris, though Bucher based his assessment
more on her jewelry than on her garments. The
single diamond brooch she wore at the base of her
throat was easily worth fifty thousand dollars.

Then there was a ring and a bracelet to match. In Bucher's opinion she had damn poor taste—and even poorer judgment. He could rattle off the names of half a hundred hoods right here in New York who'd burn her in public to get their hands on her jewelry. She made as if to scoot over, giving him room to sit, when she noticed his approach. Bucher did not waste time on preliminaries.

"You wanted to see me, Maude Ann?" he asked as he sat beside her.

She nodded silently, studying his hard face with cautious eyes. "I—it's about this morning. When I first saw you—when we saw each other. Bucher . . ." She placed a small hand on his arm, her eyes begging him. "I don't have much ready cash right at present—but I can get some, a few thousand, on occasion . . ." The words trailed off to nothing and she sat staring at him helplessly. Bucher suppressed the laughter that gathered in his throat.

"You mean to buy me off?" he asked. "To pay me blackmail to keep me from squealing that you once worked for me?"

She nodded jerkily, fighting back the tears, lower lip aquiver. "I'm—he's—my husband—we're so happy—" She sighed heavily. "It would kill Charles if he ever learned of my past."

"Working for me?"

She nodded, whispering, "Yes. For you." Her hand went impulsively to his arm. Bucher, I can pay some—"

"Why?" Bucher glanced at his chronograph. There were things he should be about, and here he was whiling away the time with a doxy turned matron.

"Why?" She sounded incredulous. "Because—"

"Maud Ann, we're both playing in better leagues these days. The rules and regulations of years ago are no longer in effect. You don't owe me anything. Not a dime. Neither now nor later. As for me telling that you once worked for me, forget it. Has it not occurred to you that I may not want to be known as a one-time whoremaster?"

Her relief was a pitiful thing to see, even mingled as it was with admiration for him, and had he not been so pressed for time, he might have felt noble. As it was, he stood.

"Forget the past," he told her. "It's dead as yesterday's headline. Today will take care of itself, so only tomorrow counts. Okay?"

She nodded, sniffing, fighting back the tears, and before he knew what she was about she had leaned forward, seized his hand, and pressed it to her lips.

"Aw for crud sake!" He jerked his hand free. "See you around, huh?" He spoke as he moved to the sidewalk near the bench where she remained seated and fell in behind a large, raw-boned woman whose arms were loaded with packages from a shopping trip. Bucher had not taken half a dozen steps when one of these packages, unnoticed, worked free and fell to the sidewalk. He stooped quickly to retrieve it, heard the almost

120

inaudible *swish* followed by the sudden meaty *thock*, then an animal grunt of surprise and a scream of pain. The raw-boned woman stood motionless, the packages around her feet, both arms flung high and wide in a crucified stance, the short, thick haft of the cross bolt protruding from her back. Slowly she turned, swinging around with lumbering pace, face stark and raw with agony, eyes bulging. Her hands were still raised when she pitched backward and lay still.

Bucher was nowhere near the woman when she fell to the sidewalk, but some twenty yards away behind a second fountain, cold eyes studying the direction from which the crossbow bolt had come, knowing it had been meant for him and not for the woman who'd gotten it. Instinctively, he cast a cold glance to where Maud Ann gaped in mingled surprise and disbelief. As he watched, she rose quickly and hurried from the scene, which, after another few seconds of trying to see from where the bolt had been fired, he did also, though in a different direction, the sounds of alarm from the crowd gathering around the fallen woman ringing in his ears. One thing was for certain. He wanted no delay with the police. Although White Hat would spring him in a matter of minutes, Bucher felt he did not have those minutes to waste. Already he had wasted too much time on Maud Ann Billingsley. He was hurrying toward a cab stand some seconds later when a thought jerked him up short:

Could Maud Ann have engineered the setup to have him knocked off?

Virtually the same instant the question posed itself, Bucher washed it from his mind as ridiculous. There had been only one thing on the mind of the woman he had known as Maud Ann Beeker years ago, and that one thing was his assurance that he would not divulge details of her lurid past. An assurance he had willingly given, Bucher reflected dourly, though it had damn near cost him his life. But if not Maud Ann, then who?—and Bucher knew no amount of reasoning could possibly bring him to acuse her of the crime. White Hat's director? This was beyond consideration. It was not only ridiculous; it was simpleminded. And yet only White Hat's director and Maud Ann Billingsley, née Beeker, had known he would keep an appointment with Maud Ann, or the location of that appointment. Correction! Only White Hat's director had known! Maude Ann had merely requested the meeting and given the location where Bucher could find her, but the young woman had not known he would keep the appointment, nor at what hour. Therefore, Bucher reasoned, someone else, a third person, had known he would meet Maud Ann, and the time he would do so. But who, dammit?

"I be goddamn!" Bucher said aloud, suddenly remembering. Of course! Ahmed Fowzie had rigged the setup to kill him, because Fowzie had a bug on the Pink Pussycat's telephone, over which he had talked with Fowzie, and only seconds later had talked to the director, who'd informed him of Maud Ann's desire for a meeting and the place it was to be held. Bucher's conversation with the director over the Pink Pussycat's phone had been in the ancient and extinct Serbo-Croatian dialect, but this would prove no insurmountable obstacle to a mastermind criminal of Fowzie's caliber— a point he must remember to inform White Hat on.

"I've been grossly underestimating that sonofa-bitch," Bucher growled to himself as he entered the cab.

"Hey-hey!" the cabby said without mirth as he noted the citizens band transceiver Bucher carried. "You got one too, eh?" And he lifted one similar to Bucher's from the front seat beside him. "Most everybody's gettin' one these days. Range ain't more'n fifteen miles, but man, that covers New York City like a blanket, hey? Where to, Mack? You ain't said."

Paradoxically, at that instant, Bucher remembered his meeting with Lupo "the Tiger" Sinetto and the two specific points he'd intended questioning Sinetto on. The first, Leo Natoni; the second, information concerning the five kidnapped Israelis. He'd become so enamored with the idea of the Syndicate lifting the quarter of a million dead-only hit price for keeps that he'd simply forgotten to grill Sinetto about the Israelis and Natoni. Information concerning Natoni was of no major importance, but information concerning the Israelis was, and, since Sinetto usually kept

123

his finger on the crime pulse of the city, the man would likely know of any current rumors concerning the Israelis making the rounds of the underworld. It was worth a try, anyway. And this time he would not forget, Bucher promised himself.

"Bozeman's Bar," he told the cabby, giving the man the address, though in no wise certain why he chose the place. Still, it had a phone, was not too distant, and was never crowded. He'd call Sinetto from there. And Kleyr.

Bucher was not prepared for the surprise that greeted him when he walked into Bozeman's Bar a bit later, and responded, although silently, with his characteristic: "I be goddamn."

"Don't look so dismayed," Sharon Szold smiled from back of the bar. Across the room opposite her, in one of the booths, sat two young men mulling over beers, each with a suspicious bulge beneath his jacket and each with a guitar case within easy reach on the floor beside him.

"I've got a right to look dismayed," Bucher said. "What the hell goes on here? Where's Boze?"

"If you mean Mr. Curdi, he's in back lying down, recovering from a seizure of nerves; I gave him a sedative to calm him down." Sharon nodded toward the two across the room. "And they're with me. My cousins, Mike and Ike."

With a definite feeling of being had, Bucher blurted: "The hell you say."

"Well, it's almost true." She laughed, enjoying herself. "Mike and Ike are their JDL names. That's Mike on the left, Ike on the right." She

124

spoke to the two young men. "Okay, fellows, front and back, and don't let anyone get past you unannounced while Mr. Bucher is here."

They nodded, smiling at Bucher as they went to obey, and he stood looking first after one then the other, noting that the snap latch of each guitar case was open, the cases held shut only by two fingers of the hand that carried it.

"I'd still like to know what'n hell's going on." Bucher sat himself at the bar opposite Sharon.

"Rabbi Shimesh."

"He sent you back?"

"That's right. And with reenforcements. After that trick you pulled on the two Al Fat'ha and got them to blow themselves to smithereens, then bested the others who'd come to kill you, but especially—" She burst out laughing, her throaty contralto already sending tingly prickles squiggling along Bucher's spine, and continued laughing, looking at him, until the infectious merriment became overly contagious and he, too, commenced laughing, but sobered abruptly.

"What the hell're we laughing at?" he demanded. "What's so funny?"

"Your bilking the Wog out of fifteen thousand dollars. Ali Annaser is in a tight bind because of it. He must either recover the fifteen thousand, and take your head as interest, or his own people will execrate him. A fact not generally known is that of all Orientals, with the Arab, saving face or regaining face is the most vital. Did you know it?"

"Oh, yes, though one doesn't normally think of the Arab as an Oriental."

"This one doesn't think of Ali Annaser without getting a bad taste in her mind," Sharon said, pointing to herself. "I hope the Secretary of State hurries and gets Egypt and Israel to sign that peace pact. If Egypt signs, all the other Arab nations of the Middle East will follow along."

"I be very damn!" Bucher said emphatically. "And all along I've been wondering why, just at this particular pinpoint in time, all this Israeli-Arab hassle had to break out. So why is the story of Nabil Chehade Shazar's will leaving Israel and the U.S. plans for constructing a simple hydrogen motor just now making the news media? Shazar has been dead for weeks. Or is it months now?"

"I don't know why the story is just now making the news," Sharon Szold said, though refusing to meet Bucher's eyes as she said it.

"And that news yarn about Israel having those atomic weapons—"

"That isn't a yarn," Sharon interrupted. "And I'm in a position to know, though if you quote me as having said it I'll lie like a trooper and deny everything." She eyed him intently behind a fetching grin. "I take it you haven't heard the latest."

"Floor me with surprise."

"It's called 'multi-plasmid hydrocarbon-degrading pseudomonas."

"Huh?" He couldn't help it. It just slipped out.

Then: "Okay. I'm floored by surprise. What is it?"

"An oil-eating bug. Microbes really. Microbes that can, and do, devour oil at a fantastic rate."

"Yeah. That's right. Now tell me that Israel microbiologists have invented or discovered or done whatever one does to get these little oil-eating animals, and threaten to loose them through the Arabian oil fields of the world."

Sharon shook her head. "An American microbiologist developed them. An American microbiologist working for one of the large food chains. He was searching for a 'friendly' microbe that would destroy the deadly salmonella bacteria, which thrive in a non-oxygen environment, and developed the oil-eating bug instead." The laughter was still in her voice as she continued. "But the Arabs aren't too stupid to read the handwriting on the wall—now that Israel has developed the same strain of oil-eating bacteria."

"Yeah," Bucher said again, feeling somewhat foolish, yet believing her nonetheless. "All of which further complicates a mess already too damn complicated to untangle. The Arabs already know Israel has the oil-eating bug?"

"I suppose. It's been published on all the networks. About half an hour ago."

"Okay, okay, since things can't get any damn tougher . . . So what the hell happened to Boze Curdi?"

"He's in back; he lives in a room in back. The doctor left just before you arrived. When Mike and Ike and I arrived he was having a nervous

127

breakdown, or some sort of fit, or something awful. I managed to find a doctor's phone number in his wallet and called him. He gave me some medicine to give Curdi—but I can't remain here and tend to him if you leave."

"Duty to the cause first."

"That's exactly right. My first duty is to the cause of my people."

"Good girl." Bucher nodded approval.

"Should it occur to you to do so, Mr. Bucher, you may notice that I'm not a girl."

"Oh, yes. I've noticed. Several times. Christ, you think I'm blind? Or made of wood?"

Sharon laughed happily. "And I was only teasing when I told you I'd warned Kleyr she'd best be on her guard lest I take you from her. But Kleyr knows this."

"Yeah," Bucher said, not listening, thoughts busy with his reasons for returning to Bozeman's Bar as he looked over a shoulder at the pay telephone on the wall behind him. Still without answering her, he left the bar and walked to it. First to call Lupo Sinetto for info about the kidnapped Israelis and also about one Leo "Bang-Bang" Natoni, and then he'd call Kleyr; she'd probably chew him out for having neglected to call her before now. As before, when he dialed the number Curdi had told him belonged to Lupo Sinetto, Gunboat Dru answered, his raspy old voice coming over the wire like the rattle of rusty tin pipes. Then he recognized Bucher's voice.

"Butcher! Man, you sure don't give a body

much time. Them twelve hours you give the boss to get results in ain't up yet." His voice descended to a conspiratorial whisper. "But I'll tell you one thing, Bucher. He shore as hell is workin' on the big boy to get that hit price on your worthless noggin lifted for keeps. And you know something, son? He just might succeed at it, too. You gotta give ol' Lupo credit when credit's due, Bucher, hell. You can't—"

"Gunboat," Bucher cut in. "For Christ's sake slow down. I'm not calling about the hit price. What's the latest word about the five Israelis that were kidnapped in broad open daylight this morning?"

Dru's voice was cagey when he replied. "Whadda ya mean what's the latest word. This on the level?"

"It's on the level, Gunboat. You know I wouldn't try to con an old trooper like you."

"Yeah—uh—the hell you wouldn't, you young whippersnapper. But anyway, there ain't no latest word."

"And what is that supposed to mean?"

"Just what I said, Butchy. Honest. I swear it. I've already made about four dozen calls tryin' to learn the latest word on the kidnappin's myself and ain't learned nothin'. I mean absolutely nothin'—so it musta been Ahmed Fowzie that pulled the job. Or had it done."

"Why do you say that?"

"On account of he's the only one operatin' in the boss's territory with enough moxie, or little

129

enough sense, to cross Lupo Sinetto, that's why I say that. Fair enough?"

"Fair enough," Bucher replied, disappointed. "Now what about Leo Natoni?"

"Bang-Bang Natoni? Okay, Butchy, so what about the nogood sonofabitch?"

"Where do I find him?"

"That I can't help you with neither. I ain't seen the rat in months. Not since he quit the boss. But when and if you find him, I hope you bust his face in."

"Because he walked out on Lupo?" Bucher asked, guessing. Bozeman Curdi had claimed rumor had it that Natoni had died three years ago in a munitions manufacturing plant blast down in Georgia.

"'At's perzactly right," Gunboat declared. "On account of he walked out on the boss without a by-your-leave, kiss-my-ass, ner nothin'. Just took a powder without nary a word to nobody."

Bucher thanked the old mobster and hung up, fished through his pockets for a dime to call Kleyr, and when he found none, returned to the bar for change.

"Pssssst!" This from the JDL member guarding the front door.

"What is it, Ike?" Sharon Szold asked tightly.

"It's Jody Zahrene," Ike replied. "She just parked across the street."

"Alone?"

"Yes. Alone."

"Then take a booth and play drunk," Sharon

told him, hurriedly unhooking the Star of David from about her neck and dropping it in a pocket.

"Clue me." Bucher told her.

"Jody Zahrene is the Wog's one and only heartthrob. Or at least was until she made the big time. You may know her as Cheryl Candaux."

"The movie actress?"

Sharon nodded, eyes on the front entrance. "The Wog discovered her a few years ago, doing bit parts for a rundown acting troupe that couldn't afford to pay her anything except in experience, so he took her under his wing. To give the devil his due, Ali Annaser knows how to direct a play, how to train an actor to get the very best results possible. He's discovered several 'name' actors in that theater he runs and Cheryl Candaux is one of them."

"Won't she recognize you? You aren't exactly an unknown, you know."

"I hope she doesn't. At least not until we find out what she's doing here."

Swiftly Bucher moved around the end of the bar and toward a door behind Sharon that led to the back.

"Where are you going?"

"This ugly mug of mine isn't exactly unknown either," Bucher grinned. "Especially in certain circles to which Cheryl Candaux may belong, Hollywood notwithstanding." He stepped through the open doorway, turned out of sight from the bar proper, and stood watching. In a booth across the room Ike sprawled in drunken relaxation, discussing metaphysics waggishly with an invisible associate. Sharon made a quick gesture toward the rear, where Mike stood watching her questioningly, in his hands a short-barreled, vicious automatic rifle, and at her gesture he vanished silently out back again.

"Here she comes." This from Sharon, whispered, spoken without turning. And she was right.

Cheryl Candaux had never performed for her millions of movie fans a more casual yet graceful entrance onto the screen than the one she performed for those watching as she entered Curdi's Crudhouse. Willow slender, neat, her dress immaculate in its simplicity, consciously or not, she projected the epitome of queenly poise as she paused immediately inside the door, surveyed the room briefly, then commenced searching through her purse for a coin as she walked toward the pay phone.

"Jesus," Bucher said to himself from the dimness of the storeroom in which he stood. "This is my day to meet living dolls." First Sharon Szold, now Cheryl Candaux—he could not think of her as Jody Zahrene.

Without giving Sharon any more notice than any movie queen gives a barmaid, the newcomer placed a quarter on the counter with: "Change, please."

Sharon gave her change for the phone without comment and watched as the woman went to the pay phone, fed it, and dialed. When the party on the other end answered, she spoke softly in Arabic,

132

but in the quiet Bucher heard each single word she uttered.

"There is no one here at the bar, darling Ali." It was the way she said it that reached Bucher hardest. She spoke as if she were addressing a very special god—and if it was Ali "Wog" Annaser to whom she spoke, she was certainly still available to be his one-and-only heartthrob, as Sharon had described the woman, big-time actress or not. Of course none of those listening to her could hear the response she received, though Bucher already suspected her to be on a scouting mission. This suspicion was strengthened by her reply of:

"But Ali, dearest, the bar is empty except for one very youngish man, who is exceedingly intoxicated, and the barmaid."

Although Bucher could not distinguish the words which came over the phone, he did manage to recognize the voice of Ali Annaser. The man was in a screaming rage, and after a moment's listening to him, Cheryl Candaux spun in surprise from the wall to face Sharon Szold—who now rested with one elbow on the bar, a snub-nose .38 couched in one hand.

"Who is it you seek?"

"He . . . Ali Annaser says there is no barmaid here," the actress said woodenly. "Yet you are the barmaid."

"Who were you sent here to find?" Sharon demanded. "Quickly! Lest I pull the trigger!"

"A man," said Cheryl Candaux, hanging up the

phone with the Wog screaming hysterically into it from the other end. "A man named Bucher. I was to determine if the man was here, then notify Ali Annaser either way."

"And what did you want with this man?" Sharon insisted for Bucher's benefit.

"I was only to call Ali. That is all. Who are you? You are not a barmaid. And your face is vaguely familiar. Who are you?"

"Hold her as a hostage," Bucher said quietly from the darkened storeroom to Sharon. "But not here. The Al Fat'ha will probably show here any minute. And see if she knows where the Al Fat'ha are holding the five kidnapped Israelis."

Cheryl Candaux did not know anything of the Israelis, not even that the Al Fat'ha was supposed to have kidnapped them, and her protestations at being held hostage suddenly ceased when Ike in the booth miraculously sobered and Mike came from the rear at Sharon's summons.

"Are you going to kill me?" she pleaded hoarsely.

"Don't be silly," Sharon told her. "Just do as you are told and everything will be all right. My friends and I are taking you to a place where you will be safe and comfortable—but do as you are told." When Ike and Mike had led the actress out, Sharon turned to Bucher: "Why are we holding her? Do we need a hostage?"

"Not specifically. And not Cheryl Candaux, certainly. If word she is being held gets out, half the country will hate us. But I'm returning to the 99

134

Name theater. Keep her on ice until then, until I call you—at Rabbi Shimesh's number?"

Sharon nodded. "Or either of the other numbers I gave you."

Bucher's reason for wanting to revisit the 99 Names theater was to put Wog Annaser on the grill, because Wog Annaser, in Bucher's opinion, was at least involved in the kidnapping of the five Israelis. The fat and greasy bastard might not be the kingpin behind the snatch, but he knew about it; of this Bucher was positive. Moreover, the slob would know where the Israelis were stashed. And rescuing them was first and foremost in Bucher's thoughts. That, and discovering who had hired Leo Natoni to boobytrap the maroon Olds he had rented. Here, again, Ali "Wog" Annaser headed the bill, because he and his followers were the only ones to benefit from such a caper. Nabil Chehade Shazar willing his plans for the hydrogen motor to the governments of Israel and the United States had placed the Al Fat'ha, and the entire Arab world that depended on crude petroleum, in a tight bind. But neither Israel nor the U.S. would deal with the Al Fat'ha as long as the Israelis were still held as kidnap victims.

Bucher was the last to leave Bozeman's bar, and before doing so he found Boze Curdi in a slovenly room in back of the storeroom, at the end of a short hall. From the look of him, Bucher suspected Curdi was unconscious from more than just the sedative Sharon had given him. The man lay sprawled on a double bed and snored viciously, on the floor beside the bed an empty whiskey bottle. There is no drunk like a backslid alcoholic, Bucher reminded himself as he pulled the bar's front door shut and left the place. Boze Curdi was on his way to skid row again, the poor bastard.

By freak happenstance or no, Bucher got the same cab he had taken from Rockefeller Plaza to come to Bozeman's.

"99 Names?" the man repeated in amazement. "That theater in the village? Hey-hey, man are they havin' a ball there—accordin' to one of my brother hacks workin' that side." He flourished his CB set at Bucher. "Great little items, this. Hey-hey!"

"What sort of a ball?" Bucher asked, at once interesed.

"No details. Just a big hassle of some sort. Bloody, too."

"Any names?"

"Yeah. One or two, but I don't recall—"

"Annaser?"

"Yeah! Come to think of it, Anus-her was one of the names."

And the other, Bucher was soon to learn, was the Jewish Defense League—which struck him as odd indeed. He had just left Sharon Szold, an important member of the League, one who would know of any planned attack by the League on Annaser and his 99 Names theater, yet she had not mentioned it. Even so, he remained in the background, watching, when he dismissed the cab some minutes later. And there was plenty to watch, even from where he stood half a block away. From such a short distance one could not miss the antics of the gargantuan Ali "Wog" Annaser.

The man wore a flowing robe of the sort Bucher had seen him wear earlier, though the present one was far more lavish and ornate, with colorful scenes embroidered on the back and sleeves, the robe itself a flowing affair that covered the quivery mountain of suet that was Ali Annaser to his very ankles. His enormous feet, long and wide and flat as a greasy spoon's griddle, flapped on the hard concrete as he leapt and careened about in front of his 99 Names theater, the huge front double doors of which had been apparently splintered by a small hand bomb placed at the base of them.

"It is a fiendish plot of Jewry to discredit me and my 99 Names establishment," Ali Annaser shrieked, flopping lugubriously about from one policeman to the other, waves of fat surging and receding beneath the robe—which caused Bucher to wonder absently if the man could do an about face inside his thick sheath of rubbery suet without the sheath itself revolving. The man was in a veritable tizzy, and he flopped about here and there, screeching to any and all who gave some appearance of listening to him that the Jewish Defense League was behind the attack on his theater.

"It's Jews!" Annaser wrung his hands in despair. "The curse of the world—Jews, and their hydrogen motors and their oil-eating bugs and their atomic bombs poised ready to blast any friendly, peace-loving Arab neighbor off the face of the earth!"

This was a bit much for some of the onlookers, and Annaser was answered by catcalls and hoots of derision from numerous quarters, which seemed to further infuriate the lard-assed sonofabitch. He commenced to scream vilifications on all things Semitic, apparently oblivious of the fact, or at least for the time choosing to ignore it, that he was himself of Semitic ancestry, and as his vilifications grew in volume they grew proportionately in filth until a square-jawed police captain elbowed him forcefully in the gut.

"Shut up!" the officer snarled. "Zip that cave-size mouth of yours else I run you in."

"And now police brutality," Annaser wailed to the heavens at large. "Bombed, beaten, my very life threatened by stinking Jews and now police brutality!" But the policeman's order had taken the acid-bite off the man's diatribe and he began listening to those who now closed in around him who, from their garb, were members of the troupe who had been rehearsing when the disturbance began. Gradually they began coaxing the Wog back toward the shattered doors of the theater—and it was here that Bucher noticed a curious thing. Or rather, he found his eyes focused on one particular member of this troupe.

She was not dressed like those who had been rehearsing the play, for they, both men and women, wore the garb of the desert Arabs. She wore only faded jeans, a much-too-large shirt of blue denim, and a pair of sandals, hand made from goat skin by their looks. For a long minute Bucher studied the small figure, then moved toward her with a power and determination motivated by he wasn't certain what, only that he could not resist it. He was within feet of her when their eyes met, locked, and, at her negative grimace, he stopped and turned as she quickly left those around Ali Annaser and walked rapidly down the street in the direction of the villagers' Greenwich Village. They had turned the corner and Bucher had caught up with her; they were well out of sight of the 99 Names theater when she turned on him.

"Why did you interfere?" Kleyr Boriquen demanded hotly.

"What in hell are you doing away from the Carlton?" Bucher demanded savagely, through clenched teeth, in return.

"I asked first," she pouted prettily, obviously bent on beguiling him from his anger over her truancy. He seized her, though not roughly, by the shoulders.

"I asked what in hell you're doing away from the Carlton?" he gritted, shaking her gently.

For a moment she almost told him the whole truth, but decided against it; Boo lived in a world rife with dangers, and she saw little point in multiplying them. "I—I thought I might be able to help, some," was all she said. With a tiny, self-effacing smile. And waited.

"You thought you could help by joining Wog Annaser and his bunch of punks!"

"So? And I would have succeeded if you had not happened along."

"Kleyr . . . for Christ's sake!" he ended helplessly. "Holy Jesus God's very eyeballs." And stood looking at her helplessly, for the moment actually not knowing which way to turn. Then, paradoxically, as they stood there staring at one another furiously, they burst into laughter.

"We'll have to get off the street," Bucher said at last, looking hurriedly about them. "This is Arabian turf and we're way off limits."

"My transportation," Kleyr said, pointing down the street in the direction they'd been walking. "A camper. I rented it. Wog and his people think I'm a gypsy."

"But why?" Bucher demanded again, some seconds later, as they got into the front of the camper.

"I told you, Boo. I thought I might help. And maybe I have. A little."

"How?"

"Well." She smiled at him in mock mystery. "I know who tried to kill you by blowing up your rented Oldsmobile."

"Bang-Bang Natoni?"

"You know?"

"I do now. Who sicced Natoni onto me?"

"The Wog. As a revenge measure. In hopes of

140

saving his face for your having bilked him and the Al Fat'ha out of fifteen thousand dollars. There is some talk that Annaser's leadership of the Al Fat'ha might be turned over to Ahmed Fowzie because of the fifteen thousand, and the Wog is about to lose his marbles because of it."

"And the fifteen thousand dollars is the only reason? The Wog's people have been after me all day."

"That, and of course Ahmed Fowzie has issued orders you must be killed, but you know this."

"Ain't it the goddamn truth," Bucher growled. "Come on. Get this thing started. We can't hang around this neck of the woods. Where do I find Leo Natoni, by the way?"

"Why, at the 99 Names ... you didn't see him? Dressed as a Bedouin? The one with the gimpy leg? And the—face?"

"That was Natoni? What the hell happened to his face?"

Kleyr pulled the camper out into the intermittent traffic before replying. "An explosion, I think. Or so I overheard from two of the girls in the troupe. Down in Georgia somewhere, I believe. It almost killed the man, but plastic surgery managed to make him look human again. Almost." She shuddered. "One of the girls thinks he's cute."

"Drive back around to the 99 Names," Bucher told her. "Circle around and let me out; then keep circling. I won't be long."

"Boo—"

141

"Do it!"

"Yes, Boo."

If Bucher noticed her ready submissiveness, he gave no comment that it was thoroughly out of character with her, for his thoughts were busy with the possibility of Lupo Sinetto getting the quarter of a million dead-only reward lifted off his head for keeps. If Sinetto succeeded, then he would owe the man one. A big one. For the lifting of the hit price also meant he would shed White Hat like a wet blanket, and he and Kleyr would retire to her place in Arecibo, Puerto Rico, and ...

By the time Kleyr tooled the camper around to the front entrance of the 99 Names theater the crowd that had been there previously was dispersed, with only a very few stragglers yet remaining. And none of these gave Bucher a second look as he dismounted very quickly from the vehicle and entered the theater through the splintered front doors. Once he was inside the theater, however, trouble commenced immediately. And he was prepared for it.

"Crunch!"

The individual Wog Annaser had left to guard the front entrance of 99 Names seized his smashed jaw with both hands and spun around and around, making gurgly sounds. Bucher paused momentarily, prepared to strike again, but this was unnecessary. When the man realized the extent of the damage the brass knucks had done to his face he fainted dead away, whereupon Bucher proceded. His quarry was Leo "Bang-Bang" Natoni. He wanted to know if it had been Wog Annaser or Ahmed Fowzie who ordered the bombing of the maroon Oldsmobile. True, Kleyr had said it was Annaser who had ordered the job, yet Bucher knew full well it could have been Fowzie ordering through Annaser. Either way, the means by which Annaser and Fowzie had been keeping track of his movements was little short of uncanny. Ever since beginning this caper, it seemed as if the enemy, either Fowzie or Annaser, or both, always knew where he would be and at what time. Except at the Pink Pussycat. Johnny Ungo had truly been surprised to see him at the Pink Pussycat. As surprised even as Ahmed Fowzie had been to talk to him on the phone there. So, Bucher rationalized, it was high goddamn time he was coming up with some answers. All day long he'd been futzing about hither and yon trying to get his hooks solidly in this caper. Well, as he saw it, the time had come to quit futzing around. The time had come when he wanted some answers. Straight answers, dammit! Such as the answers he intended to get from Leo Natoni.

This morning when he had visited the 99 Names theater posing as Tony Pelegroso he had seen it only from the stage end. From the opposite end, that is, from the audience end, the place looked quite different. The place was narrow, steeply sloped, and constructed in the manner of a seventeenth-century European opera house, with two lines of individual boxes, one above the other, over the primary audience area, the boxes circling

143

the entire interior of the building. Bucher took all this in at a glance. His main interest was directly ahead. On the stage. Where Wog Annaser and the cast of the play stood, listening to the grossly obese director, who stood at one end of the stage, addressing the cast on the other end.

"I be goddamn," Bucher muttered to himself. "The son of a bitch must weigh at least five hundred pounds."

Wog Annaser rippled and purled around the edges as he moved, though Bucher saw nothing odd in this. He accepted such as the way things were. Even so, he in no wise expected the Wog's garb to be as it was. The hideously gross quarter-ton of grease was practically nude.

". . . and it is in this particular scene," the Wog announced in a large and oily voice, "that we depict the inferiority of the despicable *Jew!*" He spoke the word as though it were vulgar. "It is in this particular scene that the audience begins to understand that the *Jew* is a sub-race, and infrahuman." "Furthermore, the reality of this death orgy on stage will be a high point in my directing career. The audience, of course, will think it's only acting, will not know the actress is actually dying. Realism, *realism* is the key word of today's successful theater! And of course the Butcher will come charging in, Jim Dandy to the rescue, ol' Hairbreadth Harry in person, and that's when the magnificent finale of our final act takes place. For the Butcher, also, will enact a very realistic part of our little drama—when our planted marksmen take him to final task."

Bucher, in the cool dimness of the audience section of the theater, could not be seen easily from on stage. However, he could be seen quite plainly by anyone in any of the boxes in the two tiers, which were above the stage lights, and it was while the Wog was speaking thus that, during a pause in the man's dialogue, the cry came from a box to the right of the stage . . .

"The Butcher!"

8

Glancing quickly upward, Bucher caught sight of the horribly scarred and deformed face of Leo "Bang-Bang" Natoni, author of the bleating cry, and immediately made for the stairs to his right leading up.

"The Butcher?" a woman screamed in fear—an emotion which apparently overcame most of those on the stage, for in seconds, by the time her cry diminished, the stage was bare save for the Wog and one or two of the men. The Wog, becoming obsessed as he was with the means of ridding himself of the plague known as the Butcher, commenced charging aimlessly about the stage, waving his arms and shouting at the top of his not inconsiderable lung power: "Kill the bastard! Kill him! Kill the Butcher! Fifty thousand dollars,

cash, to the man who kills the son of a bitch!"
Those who feared him seemed to have a predilection for hysteria whenever he made the scene unexpectedly. Certainly Leo Natoni was of this predilection, for as Bucher mounted the stairs and drew near the man, Natoni bleated wanly in terror. Despite his great need to talk with Natoni, Bucher almost turned away in revulsion at sight of the man's face. Little wonder Kleyr had shuddered when she spoke of it. And one of the girls here at the theater thought Natoni was cute. Dear God above!

"Make with the words, sonofabitch!" Bucher snarled savagely on reaching the man. "The right words, else I drill you here and now." As if to accent words with action, Bucher shucked his Walther—whereupon Natoni bleated wanly again. "Who sicced you onto me? Who fingered me for you? Who told you I was in a maroon Olds?"

"Bucher—please—fer t'love of God—!"

Crack! Bucher's back hand lashed across the man's face triggered another bleat, this one followed by a forlorn sob of despair.

"Words!" Bucher gritted. He thumbed back the hammer and leveled the muzzle of the Walther between the man's eyes. "Good words!"

Leo Natoni pointed, with a thumb, down toward the stage where the commotion raised by the Wog was still in progress. At the gesture, Bucher's hopes faded. He had hoped to secure from this deformed killer some link to the true identity of Ahmed Fowzie. And even possibly to find out

147

where the five kidnapped Israelis were being held, but as he read the truth in Natoni's eyes this hope faded. The old killer knew nothing of importance.

"Then what do you know?" Bucher spat, never for an instant forsaking his role of merciless killer; it was the only image Natoni could respect.

"Know about what, Bucher?"

"Ahmed Fowzie. The five kidnapped Israelis and where they're held. And who gives Wog Annaser his orders? And how?"

"He gets his orders on the phone from Fowzie, then picks up payment he's due at the post office. At least he says they're from Fowzie. It's allus on t'phone. God, this morning! When them five Jews was kidnapped. Fowzie claims he didn't order the kidnapping and the Wog claims him and the Al Fat'ha didn't have nothing to do with it either, so there was a screaming hassle on the phone. Fowzie thinking the Wog had done it and the Wog thinking that Fowzie done it, and that Fowzie was taking him and the Al Fat'ha off the payroll. The Wog got real shook. And now the word is that unless the Wog scores on you and gets his fifteen thousand dollars back the whole Al Fat'ha just might be turned over to Ahmed Fowzie. It's driving the Wog outta his nut."

"Who is Ahmed Fowzie? What does the punk look like?"

Leo Natoni shook his misshapen head. "I don't know what he looks like, Bucher. I ain't never seen the guy. I ain't never even spoke to Ahmed Fowzie but once and then that was on the phone.

It gives you the creeps, like. Sort of like talkin' to someone who's speakin' from the grave, maybe. Are you—you gonna burn me, Bucher?"

"No. Ever know of me shooting an unarmed man?"

"No, that I ain't, for a fact. Only . . . I don't care much if you do. After me boobytrappin' your Olds, I mean—no! Hell! That ain't like I wanted to say it! But look at me, Bucher. What'n hell has a body with my looks got to look forward to, huh? No, I ain't never heard of you shootin' a unarmed man. But I won't hold it agin' you if you make me the first."

"Go to hell," Bucher growled. But he did not leather his piece. Although the noise inside the 99 Names was beginning to settle down Bucher knew without being told that many of Ali Annaser's men were prowling about the place in search of him. And no bigger than the joint was, some were sure to locate him. "There's a mug mechanic down in Atlanta who specializes in problems such as yours, Leo. Name of Swan. Adam Swan. No, I don't know his address, but pay him a visit. It'll cost, but he does good work."

The other simply stared, saying nothing, overcome by emotion in realizing that the man he had tried earlier in the day to kill was now offering him a helping hand.

"Th-thanks, Bucher," he snubbed wetly. "I won't forget."

Suddenly, from the stage below, the Wog thundered in tones that shook the rafters: "He's up on

149

the first tier! Kill him! Kill him!" And in the quiet pause that followed, Bucher said loud and clear:

"Why don't you do the job yourself, you slimy, fat son of a bitch?"

The quiet pause becomes a deathly hush, a hush that prevailed until it was shattered by the Wog's gargantuan guffaw, the laughter itself indicative of the man's opinion as to what the final outcome of a hassle between him and Bucher would be. And when Bucher, above, heard the timbre of this laughter he smiled bleakly in fierce anticipation; he liked to see overconfidence in mutts about to tangle with him. Then he heard the Wog quietly issuing orders that none of his men were to interfere, that he intended to take the Butcher apart piece by little piece. Bucher descended the stairs.

The Wog stood spraddle-legged at center downstage, arms akimbo, an unwholesome smirk on his repulsive features as he watched Bucher's approach. Undeniably the man looked forward to a test of physical strength between himself and Bucher, a fact that increased Bucher's anticipation immeasurably.

"You think you can best the Wog, infidel bastard?" the man burpled greasily as Bucher mounted the stage.

"Depends on what you mean by 'best,' " Bucher replied in agreeable tones. "I don't think I can beat hell out of you, if that's what you mean."

"You don't?" The pits of suet at the bottom of

which were the Wog's eyes squirmed inquisitively. "You don't think you can best the Wog?"

Bucher was amazed by the dumb sonofabitch's stupidity. The obese lout actually believed he could come out on top of a go-down nitty-gritty. "That's right. I don't think I can best the Wog." All the time Bucher moved nearer the man, who now held out his hand.

"Very well," Ali Annaser said blandly. "But first give me back the fifteen thousand dollars you stole from me this morning." He even had little enough sense to extend a hand to receive the money. "Why is it you think you cannot best the Wog?"

"Well, at the risk of sounding childishly trite, I don't think I can because I know I can."

Bucher's vice grip closed with crushing force around the other's extended wrist, and in a single flow of power Bucher hauled forward mightily, knelt and heaved, and the gross obscenity that was Ali "Wog" Annaser sailed bodily across the stage to come to an abrupt, building-quaking halt against the wall. Surprisingly, the man was on his feet at once, but now in a quiver of maniacal rage. A rage that expressed itself in a scream of frenzied hate.

"Come on, Anus," Bucher said. "We mustn't keep our audience waiting, must we?" Swiftly he scanned the theater. True, Annaser had given his men instructions not to interfere, but Bucher had not heard these instructions in their entirety, for they may have included orders to gun him down from concealment should the hassle go against their interests—which it was at the time doing. And which Bucher was determined it would continue to do. Still, he couldn't attend to the Wog properly if someone were taking pot shots at him.

The Wog's rage shook the man all over, visibly. He was veritably aquiver with it as he lumbered toward where Bucher stood, both hands now outstretched, fingers spread to grab, to seize, to rend, to tear asunder, none of which they accomplished. Bucher did not permit them to. He moved aside, clubbed the groping hands away, braced himself, and swung with all the strength of his powerful body, bringing the fist armored with brass knucks up from shoe-top level in a devastating uppercut that connected with the underside of the Wog's overhanging paunch.

"FoooooooooFUH!" This from the leader of the Al Fat'ha as Bucher's arm buried itself to the elbow in his blubber. The Wog stood stunned, vast maw hanging open. His glazed eyes protruded dangerously from their twin caves of fat. Bucher then hammered the Wog's quivering belly and chest furiously, with both fists. The effect of this was most startling. From inside the fat man there came rumbling noises similar to those made by an overloaded freight train struggling up a steep grade. His eyes bulged even farther. Great veins stood out and throbbed angrily on his face. He made vague, pawing motions and commenced to discolor remarkably. Bucher struck again and again, burying his forearm to the elbow in the Wog's belly fat. The Wog collapsed in a heap, literally bounced off the footlights and onto the front row of seats.

"Who gave the order to have me skewered on a crossbow bolt at Rockefeller Center a bit ago?" Bucher snarled, and when the Arab didn't answer, he leaped down and raked the brass knucks brutally down the side of the man's face.

"Who sicced the three muscles onto me at Bozeman's Bar last night?" Bucher demanded, raising his hand.

"Ahmed Fowzie!" the Wog shouted, dodging, all fight gone.

"And who gave the orders to dynamite my Oldsmobile?"

"Fowzie!"

"Who ordered Johnny Ungo to machine gun me from a black limousine?"

"Fowzie!"

"And who sicced Tony Pelegroso onto me?"

"Fowz—!"

"Just as I thought, you sonofabitch. It was too amateurish. The Pelegroso thing was your idea. You led Tony astray, fatso. He'll go up the river for a long time."

"Johnny Ungo will avenge him."

"Not from hell he won't, and that's where Johnny Ungo is right now."

"He's dead?"

"I burned him." Bucher shucked his heater. He had no intention of using the Walther on the

Wog, but he had just seen one of the stage curtains move suspiciously, and if one of Annaser's killers lurked there . . .

"Y-you killed Johnny Ungo?" the Wog asked in a whisper, seemingly unable to believe it.

"You want a signed confession?"

The Wog massaged his chest with both hands, looking a bit stunned. Obviously, in his estimation, Johnny Ungo had been the top gun of all gunmen.

"Johnny Ungo dead," he mumbled thickly, oilily, to the theater at large, still not really believing.

"Right, fat boy. And Ahmed Fowzie is next. Lupo "the Tiger" Sinetto has paid me a cool half million dollars to rid the city of New York of all his competition—which also means you if you keep making an ass of yourself." Since the Wog did not know this about Sinetto was a lie, Bucher felt secure in saying it. After all, Sinetto had tried to give him half a million. "The best thing you can do," Bucher continued, "is to fold up your tents and quietly steal away until this hassle blows over. That way you might survive. Otherwise, kaput."

"Otherwise . . . kaput?" The Wog was thinking furiously. To Bucher it was plain the man had no intention of taking the advice, was at this very moment scheming on how to survive triumphantly without taking it.

On stage a huge column of heavy curtain again moved suspiciously, whereupon Bucher said:

"And if that gink hid behind those curtains

back of you so much as shows a smidgen of gun-metal blue it's kaput for you right now."

"Rizzick!" the Wog said without turning. "Put down the gun, Rizzick."

A youngster hardly more than fifteen or sixteen shoved the curtain aside and moved into view. She was petite, with small bones, had an enormous nose resembling a flesh-colored baseball and a cleft lower lip from which saliva drooled. Bucher flinched imperceptibly.

"Rizzick," Annaser continued. "This is the Butcher. He killed Johnny Ungo."

The youngster, in desert Arab garb, glowered at Bucher, drooling. For the first time he noticed the light automatic cut-down rifle in her hands, which, to judge by her attitude, she yearned to use on him.

My God, Bucher thought to himself. A psychopathic killer, yet. Scarcely in mid-teens, but a psychopathic killer already.

"Iff'n ye harmed Leo, mister, I'll kill ye anyways."

"Put it down!" the Wog screamed in sudden terror, swinging a massive paw that knocked both the girl and the automatic rifle to the floor. Then he turned to the girl in half-apology. "Wee-One, he's the *Butcher!* The man who outgunned *Johnny Ungo!*"

"Iff'n he's harmed Leo I'll kill him anyways." The girl picked herself up stolidly from the floor.

"I gave Leo the name of a doctor in Atlanta that can mend his face," Bucher said, feeling sorry for the girl. "Dr. Adam Swan. I left Leo upstairs in one of the first-tier boxes. Why don't the two of you get together? Dr. Lamb could likely help you both." But Bucher doubted she heard his last words. The girl was already off the stage and flying toward the stairs.

"'Okay, Mr. Bucher,'" the Wog said in trembly tones. "As the saying goes: 'you can't win 'em all,' and I guess I know when it's time to fold my tents and steal quietly away. I know when I'm beaten. Any suggestions?"

"This'll cost you the leadership of the Al Fat'ha."

The Wog made a gesture meant to be a shrug. "So . . . as I said; nobody can win 'em all."

Something about this rang false to Bucher, though aside from the obvious he was unable to pinpoint what that "something" was.

"My only suggestion is to clear out and wait till the storm blows over," Bucher told the man, knowing it was advice Annaser had no intention of following. Instinct told him the Wog had no plans of relinquishing the reins of power that went with leadership of the Al Fat'ha. Not to Ahmed Fowzie or anyone else. Bucher motioned with the Walther. "Right now, walk in front of me to the street entrance."

Bucher had exited into the street a minute later and was looking about for Kleyr and her camper when the horrendous woman-child scream of mingled rage and despair reached him from within, the scream followed by: "He kilt Leo! He cut

Leo's throat!" Bucher had no trouble identifying the voice. It belonged to Wee-One Rizzick, and if his suspicions were correct, someone had overheard his conversation with Leo Natoni, disapproved of what he heard, and cut the boobytrap artist's throat when Bucher had descended to the stage to face Annaser. Bucher shrugged his indifference. The death of one such as Bang-Bang Natoni would cost him no sleep. Nevertheless, Bucher shook his head, frowning. Something, somewhere, was awry. Something was completely out of kilter and he knew what it was, yet at the same time he was unable to recognize it.

Not once, for instance, had the Wog made any reference to the attack of the JDL on 99 Names. Why? Not once had he referred in any way to the attack—which only moments before had had him leaping around like a frog on a hot griddle. Why? And the Wog's sudden docility—again, why? According to Natoni, neither the Wog nor the mysterious Ahmed Fowzie had engineered the kidnapping of the five Israelis, though each thought the other guilty of the crime. But if Fowzie hadn't, and the Al Fat'ha hadn't, who the hell had? Also, why? Especially since the Al Fat'ha had, according to White Hat's director, already made identical ransom demands as the three members of the Al Fat'ha who had committed suicide by leaping off the Secretariat building at the United Nations. All of which made one thing suddenly abundantly clear, shockingly clear, in fact. Ali

"Wog" Annaser had already lost control of the Al Fat'ha but didn't know it yet.

"My god," Bucher muttered aloud as he stepped off the curb to meet Kleyr and her camper. "If the Wog discovers he's been dethroned he'll likely send those members of the Al Fat'ha loyal to him after the Jewish Defense League, who won't take one grain of crap off any Arab. . . ."

"Why so pensive, ape?" Kleyr smiled as he crawled in beside her.

"I thought goddammit I told you to stay at the apartment today!"

"Now, Boo, please don't start that again."

"Goddammit—!"

"Lover, your wounded ego is showing."

"The hell you say."

"Hummmm, but I'll say this: I think I know well enough to suspect that you've made what you consider a remarkable discovery."

"Yeah? Is it that obvious?"

"I'm not certain yet. What is it?"

"That's the hell of it, Princess; I'm not certain either."

"Well—just start talking. Maybe you'll hit upon a *mot juste* that'll trigger everything into place. Know what I mean?" Kleyr spoke while studying the late-afternoon traffic over her shoulder, waiting for an opportune moment to join it.

"Then how's this for openers? Neither Ahmed Fowzie nor the Al Fat'ha had anything to do with the five kidnapped Israelis."

158

"For openers that's fine. Go to the head of the class. Then who did the kidnapping?"

"A third party, as yet unidentified, but who plans to take over the rackets here in the city."

"All of New York City?"

"All of New York City. And probably Jersey too. And this unidentified party is playing Ahmed Fowzie and his people against Ali Annaser and the Al Fat'ha. . . ." Bucher's words trailed off as he sat frowning at nothing, thinking hard.

"And you have absolutely no idea who this third party is?" Kleyr asked.

"No idea whatsoever. Only that he owns a black limousine." Bucher then told her of his meeting with the local Syndicate chief but said nothing about the possibility of getting the quarter-million dead-only hit price on his head removed for keeps, not wanting to raise false hopes. As he talked, Bucher had been instinctively checking the camper's interior, and realized that it had to be paid for with taxpayers' money, for damn few private citizens could afford one of its class. He pointed to the phone on the dash. "And I suppose that it goes directly to White Hat?"

Kleyr nodded brightly. "Sam gave it to me."

"And I told him you had resigned from White Hat," Bucher said somewhat wearily. "He has no doubt marked me down for a fool."

Kleyr wisely chose to ignore this. "I was talking to Sam all the time you were in the 99 Names." She waited a moment. "He seems to think you're getting close to the identity of Ahmed Fowzie. He said to tell you the sepulchral quality of Fowzie's tone, when you talked to him over the phone from the Pink Pussycat, was achieved with a baffle and an old-timey echo chamber, such as those used years ago in radio. Before TV."

Bucher frowned in contemplation. "Then . . . Ahmed Fowzie could be—a woman?"

"Sam said he figured you'd see it that way. Just the echo chamber would not conceal the sex of the speaker . . ."

"But the chamber and the baffle would."

"That's what he said. He also said to tell you that Bozeman Curdi and Lorili Popjoy Lamour studied acting together under none other than the great Ali 'Wog' Annaser."

After a moment Bucher said, slowly and distinctly and with great emphasis: "I will be holy good goddamn!"

"Saaaaay, that's quite an embellishment over 'I be goddamn.' Was Sam White right about you being close to the identity of Ahmed Fowzie?"

"I'm not certain—how long have you known Sharon Szold, Kleyr?"

"Sharon Szold? Boo, you're mistaken if—"

"*How long?*"

Kleyr started in surprise. "Well—ten years. Perhaps eleven."

As she said this, Bucher was looking about at the traffic they were in, seeking a means of quick escape. "Head for Boze Curdi's bar, Princess. I intend to hold prayer with that son of a bitch. And there we separate, understand? From there

you go back to the Carlton and there you stay!
Understand?"

"Yes, Boo."

Over half an hour later, at the small neighborhood shopping center not far from Bozeman's
Bar, where Lupo Sinetto had picked him up in the
armored Pontiac earlier, Bucher dismounted from
the camper after once more instructing Kleyr to
return to his suite at the Carlton. And once more
she promised to do so, this time intending to keep
her promise, neither she nor Bucher aware of the
two cars filled with members of the Al Fat'ha,
which had trailed them from the 99 Names theater. They waited, these Al Fat'ha, lurking in the
background near the edge of the shopping center's
parking lot until Bucher was well out of sight,
before they made their move toward Kleyr and
the camper.

Bucher did not approach Bozeman's Bar from
the front, correctly suspecting the front door
would be locked, but cut right before reaching the
bar, proceeded half a block, and turned down the
alley leading to the back of the bar. His anticipation that this rear door might also be locked
also proved correct. Listening intently, ear pressed
against the back door, he faintly made out the
sound of voices from within, one male, the other
female, voices in lively disputation.

Ordinarily, picking the lock on the back door
of the bar would have taken no more than thirty
seconds, but picking this lock without making any
sound whatsoever was quite a different matter.

Late afternoon had been well on its way when he and Kleyr had left the area of 99 Names. Dusk was settling heavily over the alley when Bucher, perspiration beading his brow, eased the spring lock of the back door to the rear and felt the door give almost imperceptibly. He was ten minutes more opening the door with the sound of rusty hinges. But he at last succeeded and stepped swiftly, silently inside, to stand staring into the twin muzzles of the double-barreled shotgun in Boze Curdi's hands. The shotgun was from the days when all domestic-made weapons of its class sported two large "dog-leg" hammers. The two dog-leg hammers of Curdi's shotgun were at full cock.

"Come on in, you stupid son of a bitch," Bozeman Curdi chortled triumphantly. "We've been waiting for you for some time."

Bucher stared in surprise, though not nearly as much at the deadly weapon pointed at his chest as at the metamorphosed Boze Curdi. Physically the man seemed to have gained six inches in height. But this was the least of the changes that had taken place, for about the man there was no longer an aura of the groveling, cringing, sniveling coward and ex-alcoholic, but a determined, aggressive positivism.

"Well, well," Bucher mused quietly. "What do you know; the mouse has turned into a lion."

"I've never been anything but a lion, bastard," Curdi gloated, still triumphantly. "You and the

John Does and Richard Roes are just simple-minded, is all."

Bucher closed the door behind him as he entered, the spring lock snapping the bolt home with a solid metallic click. It was only when he faced the long and shabby barroom that he saw the woman. She wore a pantsuit of black material and a black silk scarf about her neck, but there was no jewelry in evidence. Otherwise, she looked no different than when he had seen her earlier in the day at Rockefeller Center as Mrs. Charles Latham Billingsley, or when he had known her years earlier as Maud Ann Beeker. Her clutch purse lay on the bar; in her hand was an ugly, short-barreled .32 automatic. When Bucher recognized her, the final remnants of the bizarre puzzle which had been baffling him fell neatly into place.

"And I suppose another of your pseudonyms is Lorili Popjoy Lamour," Bucher commented easily as he drew near—until she waved him with the automatic to a barstool some distance from her. She laughed shortly, a frozen, brittle sound.

"Why not?" She motioned toward Curdi, who now stood back of the bar, but with the double-barreled shotgun still aimed squarely at Bucher. "Bozo here knows all of my aliases, don't you, darling?" She slid off her stool, and for the first time Bucher noticed she wore black, spike-heel pumps. They made her look much taller than she was, but the seven-and-a-half-inch heels also made her appear to be standing on her toes.

"Including 'Ahmed Fowzie'?" Bucher asked.

Maud Ann Beeker squinted suspiciously. "Who told you I was Ahmed Fowzie?"

"Lupo 'the Tiger' Sinetto. I had a conference with him this afternoon. He's the big-time Syndicate wheel your husband Boze was supposed to catch you belly-rubbing with, which in turn supposedly put him on skid row as an alcoholic. Oh, he caught you belly-rubbing with Lupo all right, but that was the way it was planned—right? Then, again supposedly, Boze hit the bottle and you divorced him—right? But by then you already knew most of Sinetto's business locations plus names and addresses of his key personnel. At least sufficient information to take over his operation here in New York, didn't you? So after a few short months Boze recovered from his bout with the bottle, which had never actually taken place, and the two of you were all prepared to cut Lupo down, but you had to have a cover. This you got by pretending to be Arab Ahmed Fowzie, which placed you in an ideal position for manipualting the Al Fat'ha and the Jewish Defense League against one another. Without this cover, the Syndicate might have moved its top guns from all across the country into New York and held you at bay." Most of what Bucher was telling the two was only his suspicions, educated guesses, and outright fabrications, yet the fact that he was scoring heavily on all points was too obvious from their expressions to doubt.

"Who told you all this—crap?" Maud Ann demanded, her ugly little .32 steady on him.

164

"You. Lupo Sinetto. Ali Annaser. When I discovered the two of you had studied acting under the Wog, things began to fall into place. Then, when Cheryl Candaux entered the bar here some time earlier, I hid in the storeroom back there. Back of the bar. It was then I saw the telephone dial under the bar beside the sink and recalled that whenever I came into this place Boze began washing glasses, making a lot of noise to cover the sound of his dialing this bar's number on the phone dial beside the sink, then answering the ringing phone himself, which automatically rang a phone where you were located, Maud Ann, as Ahmed Fowzie. Then, as Ahmed Fowzie, you would send some of your muscles hired away from Sinetto, or some of the Al Fat'ha, here to do me in. Tch, tch, tch, how very, very crude."

"Why crude?" She really wanted to know.

"You jumped the gun. You aren't yet in control of the Al Fat'ha."

A certain weariness crept into Maud Ann Beeker's voice. "I know." And she added promptly, gritting: "But I damn soon will be."

To Boze Curdi Bucher said: "How did you know it was me out back fiddling with the lock?"

Curdi grinned fulsomely, indicating the phone, eyes bold in their evil. "The Wog called to say you were headed this way."

"The Wog knows you and your wife here thought up the Ahmed Fowzie bit in an effort to take over the Syndicate's rackets?"

"Of course not," Maud Ann cut in. "We don't

165

trust the bastard. Did Lupo really offer you half a million in cash to get rid of his competition here in New York?"

Bucher nodded. "That he did." He glanced at Boze. "And I suppose it was you who tried to skewer me on a crossbow bolt this afternoon at Rockefeller Plaza."

"Right again," Curdi grinned, becoming more anxious to pull the twin triggers of his shotgun. "But your big mistake was to interfere in the first place. Boy, are you dumb!" His grin broadened, grew maliciously evil. "That Puerto Rican piece of yours got you snowed under but good, boy. We knew an hour after the fake kidnapping that the five Israelis were stashed in the Carlton Hotel."

"And that set of fake plans for a hydrogen motor," Maud Ann said. "You actually believed that crap, didn't you?"

"Of course not," Bucher lied loyally, stunned. "I knew the plans were fake all along. As for the kidnappings, hell, I engineered them."

Maud Ann frowned, trying to determine if he lied. "Your chippy told you the plans were fake? And you knew all about the kidnappings all along?"

"I just told you I engineered the kidnappings." It was perhaps going to cost him the secrecy of his stash-out suite at the Carlton, but he continued anyway. "I keep a suite under an assumed name at the Carlton year round."

"Under what cover?" Maud Ann asked.

"A diamond merchant."

She turned to her companion in crime. "See?" she intoned triumphantly. "I told you the diamond merchant's suite was probably his." She had climbed back on her barstool some seconds earlier, and now, as she attempted to dismount from it again, the long spike heel of one pump caught in the bar rail and she almost went sprawling. Boze, reaching quickly across the bar, caught her by an arm, steadying her until she righted herself, and for one brief instant both the deadly shotgun and the wicked little pistol were, paradoxically, pointing toward each other and not toward Bucher. However, Bucher made no attempt to escape, confident he could do so any time he chose, hoping to get more information from these two. Holy Jesus God!

The kidnappings were fake, the plans for the hydrogen moter were fake, and Bucher wondered if the story about the oil-eating bugs was a fake also. Whether fake or no, he began to see the logic of the plan of Kleyr's to manipulate the Egyptians into signing a peace agreement with Israel—and it never once occurred to him that the plan, in its entirety, was not Kleyr Boriquen's doing. But . . . my god! Mentally he staggered.

"And who doped the hashish with LSD-3 and fed it to three of the Al Fat'ha?" he asked, whereupon Maud Ann laughed merrily.

"All the Al Fat'ha loyal to that lard-assed Annaser will be doped on LSD-3 next time they take any of his hash. I discovered where his secret cache is and doped it all with LSD-3—which doesn't bode too good for you, Butcher, since they've got your chippy."

"*What?*"

Boze Curdi and Maud Ann looked at each other and laughed knowingly.

"You see," Maud Ann explained with vast patience, "I managed to manipulate the Wog and his people one last time—thanks largely to LSD-3. You get the blame for his losing leadership of the Al Fat'ha, but since he can't get at you in person, he intends to get at you through your chippy, that little two-bit Puerto Rican tart you're so gah-gah over."

A chill wave of apprehension washed over Bucher. "And how does Annaser plan to get to me through Kleyr?"

"Oh he will, believe me. He intends to fling her off the top of the Secretariat building at the United Nations, and on nationwide television yet." She spoke to Curdi. "Switch the set on, dear. Let's see if the news media have picked up the story yet." She turned brightly back to Bucher. "And before the furor of the incident dies down, my people will have moved in and rubbed Lupo 'the Tiger' Sinetto and his few remaining gunsels off the face of the earth."

Bucher nodded, understanding. Who would notice the death of a few gangsters with the nation still stunned by the brutal murder of the world-renowned Dr. Kleyr Maria Boriquen? A terrible, engulfing nausea lurched greasily in

Bucher's bowels. Moreover, with Kleyr a Jew, the Jewish Defense League would run amok in the Arab sections of the city and . . . Bucher looked at the two with guns on him. Curdi had turned the TV back of the bar on and the set was warming rapidly.

"How did the Wog's people get Kleyr?" he asked woodenly, about to make his play for freedom. If he could break free now, there might yet be time to save Kleyr, to intercept the Wog's insane scheme.

"They saw you leave 99 Names and followed, taking her when you left her and the camper at the shopping center."

During the next fifteen seconds events happened so swiftly even Bucher, with his lightening-quick reflexes, was hard put to keep up. But again Maud Ann attempted to step down from her barstool and again the long spike heel of one of her pumps caught on the bar rail. She reeled sideways, waving the small .32 automatic. This time, however, when Boze Curdi reached out to steady her, he almost missed, catching her by the jacket roughly, jerking her, and the small automatic in her hand spat angrily. A fraction of a second later the double-barreled shotgun thunder rocked the barroom— and Bucher stared, incredulous. Maud Ann's firing the automatic had been pure accident, as had been the .32 caliber hole that appeared in Boze Curdi's forehead, and Curdi's dropping the shotgun on the bar had caused the double blast, the twin loads of double-ought buckshot that tore off Maud Ann's head also an accident. Yet Bucher's surprise endured scant seconds—he had far more important things to do than mull over the quirk of fate that had ridden the city of Ahmed Fowzie. He strode with never a second glance at the two bodies on the barroom floor toward the pay phone halfway down the length of room and was dialing White Hat when there came a furious pounding of fists on the front door.

"Bucher! Bucher!" a feminine voice cried. "It's me! Sharon Szold!"

Bucher hurried to the door and jerked it open. She seized him by the coat front and literally pulled him through the door.

"Hurry!" she gasped. "There's a police helicopter waiting in that blocked-off section of the street where your Oldsmobile was bombed. Mr. White arranged everything. I'll pilot the plane myself; he's to act as a sort of central headquarters and coordinate things."

"Hey, wait a minute!" Bucher pulled back. "What'n hell's going on here?"

"It's Kleyr!" Sharon re-seized his arm and commenced pulling him back into the bar. "She's in terrible danger!" They stopped near the end of the bar, Sharon pointing toward the television. "See?"

"Oh my god!" Bucher froze, stared, transfixed.

The television cameraman was shooting from one of the large apartment buildings above the Secretariat building at the United Nations and beside the East River. Very gradually he was moving in, getting closer to the top of the Secretariat, but already the scene was shockingly graphic: the Wog was charging about, apparently shouting orders to his couple of dozen cohorts—but it was out from the parapet surrounding the roof of the building where Bucher's gaze locked. Out about twenty or twenty-five feet. The diving board, or what appeared to be a diving board, had one end lashed by an intricate network of ropes to one of the housings topping the nearest elevator shaft, and on the other end, approximately twenty feet from the edge of the parapet, on the opposite end of the diving board, stood Kleyr Boriquen. She wore only a white bra and briefs and she stood with hands held close to her side, face to the night sky. From Bucher's suddenly parched lips came the sound of mortal agony to be heard from a man innocently convicted on hearing his sentence of death.

"Wh-what is the Wog's intention?" he heard himself ask hoarsely.

"He claims he intends to sacrifice her in recompense for the three Al Fat'ha who were forced to leap from the Secretariat building earlier." She pointed toward the two bodies at the far end of the bar. "Who're they?"

"Ahmed Fowzie—either one or both." Bucher spoke without removing his eyes from Kleyr and not knowing he spoke in a rusty whisper. "There might be a chance of saving her."

"The sky sail? David's with it; he fell in love with the thing. He's with it at that small airport

171

where Mr. White ordered it taken. And that police helicopter is waiting to take us. In ten minutes we can be there."

"Us?" Bucher spoke over his shoulder plunging through the doorway.

"I'm your pilot."

9

"Look," David Szold said to Bucher with obvious enthusiasm in spite of the seriousness of the situation. "These auxiliaries. I've added them since this morning. They increased the glide ratio from six to one to eleven to one."

"David," Sharon said in quiet urgency. "We have only a little time."

"Yes. Yes, of course." For the next several minutes he spoke quietly, explaining how the sky sail could be banked sharply, now either left or right instead of just right as it had been earlier; how, by using the feet, the angle of glide could be increased or decreased abruptly; and the stabilizers, his latest addition, and the manner in which they functioned and how they could be used most advantageously. "But there may not be too

173

much time to manipulate them. Do you fly the same path you had planned to fly earlier? This morning? To rescue the guard?"

"Right," Bucher told him. "Except I must make a wider bank to the right than I'd planned in order to reach Kleyr."

"That is your intention? To grab her bodily off the end of that diving board and plunge onto the roof of the Secretariat building?"

"Do you see any other way?"

"No." David Szold shuddered. "My god, man. You don't stand a chance. Neither of you." He handed Bucher a plastic-visored helmet. "After Sharon called I wired this up to a small transceiver you can carry inside your shirt. It'll protect your face and eyes from the plane's prop-blast."

"What kind of plane is it?" Bucher asked Sharon.

"An Otter. Twin engine. It's the only one available that'll make that six-hundred-foot climb so swiftly after passing under those bridges over the East River. Except for the new jets. And you couldn't follow in the sail behind one of those." She hesitated a moment uncertainly, then: "Bucher, do you think you should do this? Attempt this? I mean . . ." Her words trailed off in confusion.

"Kleyr will be expecting me." Bucher grinned wryly. "If I don't make it, well, then, we won't make it together."

Tears sprang into Sharon's lovely eyes and her brother David turned quickly away, cursing softly

174

to himself in rank admiration at Bucher's casual regard for his incredible courage and daring.

"Hey-hey!" Bucher biffed her chin gently, then fitted the helmet over his head and placed the small transceiver inside his shirt, adjusting the earphones. "No tears. Get that Otter ready. How the hell do I get off the ground in that sail?"

"A bicycle," David said, returning to where they stood and taking each by the arm, turning them. "There. Back of the sail." He spoke to his sister. "Take off as fast as possible. The cable connecting the plane and the sky sail is of nylon and will stretch considerably under stress without breaking. Lift off quickly. Bucher, on the bicycle behind you, will follow along without a hitch." He added lamely to Bucher, "This is the only part of the operation I'm certain of."

"But the Wog and his people used helicopters to reach the roof of the Secretariat," Sharon insisted desperately. "Why can't *we* use helicopters?"

"Not fast enough," Bucher informed her. "That TV commentator said someone was standing by at the base end of the diving board to cut the ropes in case of a rescue try. From his description of the person, my guess is that it's a character named Wee-One Rizzick, a fifteen-year-old kid."

"A twenty-eight-year-old woman who looks like a fifteen-year-old brat, you mean. Her real name is Nelly Zahrene; she's Jody Zahrene's twin sister. Yes, twin to the beautiful Cheryl Candaux, who, incidentally, is being held at JDL headquarters.

Bucher! Could we not barter with the Wog? Trade Cheryl Candaux for Kleyr, perhaps . . ." She ceased talking, looking from Bucher to her brother. "But why not?"

"Because Annaser and his mutts are loaded on hashish doped with LSD-3; I'll explain what that means later. Right now let's get airborne."

A few minutes later, Bucher, holding his feet free of the madly whirring bicycle pedals, saw the Otter leave the tarmac and pulled back on the sail's elevator, feeling the tug of the harness when the sail followed suit.

"If you pull this off successfully," Bucher said to himself as the earth was swept swiftly from beneath him, "consider yourself the luckiest son-ofabitch alive."

Once he though he heard another aircraft close by, then decided it was only his imagination; though right now was not the time for an over-active imagination to put in an appearance. He did not look down at the earth and its blankets of night lights flowing away beneath him, though this was not because he feared to look down, but because it would interfere with his concentration, and concentration was the determining factor of rescuing Kleyr Boriquen. Nor was he concerned with other aircraft in the area. It had been sealed off completely; there was little chance of a repetition of the incident that had caused the three Al Fat'ha to fling the guard from atop the Secretariat and jump after him. Quite truthfully, Bucher did not give a tinker's damn how many

Al Fat'ha leaped to their deaths off the Secretariat building. The sole remaining purpose of his existence was to rescue Kleyr. He even refused to think beyond that. First Kleyr's safety, then ...

"Bucher?" Sharon's voice, coming over the small transceiver, sounded tinny, mechanical. "Bucher, can you read me?"

"I read you."

"We are coming in over the East River soon. North headed south."

"Right."

"I—just wanted you to know." Pause. "We're swinging far to the east in order not to attract attention. My signal to you that we're heading down to go under the bridges will be: 'under the bridges.'"

"Okay. Just make sure you reach a six-hundred-foot altitude by the time we're even with the southern facade of the Secretariat building. Otherwise we're spinning our wheels." Which was the same as saying: otherwise Kleyr is lost.

From the corner of his eye Bucher could see the powerful floodlights police had moved into the United Nations area; there had been no hope of preventing the news media, film outfits, and the like from becoming aware of the incident, especially not since the three Al Fat'ha had killed the guard and jumped to their deaths earlier in the day.

Bucher's plan was simplicity itself. Once under the bridges of the East River, the plane would climb, taking the sky sail with it, and, at a height of six hundred feet, he would cut loose from the plane, bank the sail sharply, and glide in onto the roof of the Secretariat building, seizing Kleyr off the diving board in passing and taking her with him. He had little doubt he could accomplish this; handling the sky sail was no problem and David Szold had assured him the banking mechanism of the sail would function properly; therefore, as Bucher saw it, the only difficulty could come from Wee-One Rizzick, who stood, with huge machete drawn, at the base end of the diving board, prepared and anxious to cut the rope that would send Kleyr plunging five hundred and fifty feet to certain death:

In that peculiar way the human mind sometime is wont to function, Bucher found himself briefly contemplating the almost incredible ease with which Maud Ann Beeker had fooled him by using two identical black limousines; it simply had never occurred to him that there might be two. Nor had it occurred to him that old rum-dum Boze Curdi might be an accomplished actor playing the part of the servile, terrified ex-alcoholic. Still—

"Bucher!" It was Sharon again.

"What?"

"Under the bridges! Good luck!"

"Yeah!" Through the plastic face-plate of his helmet Bucher watched the aged Otter tilt sharply downward and hoped David Szold's estimate that the sky sail would hold up under an air speed of two hundred miles per hour was correct, because

178

if it wasn't, it was now too late to do anything about it. They were under the first bridge before Bucher realized it, the second was behind them with equal speed, the third and last—

Then the Otter was climbing, savagely, both motors whining in protest, straining, props chewing at the air in desperate effort to attain the correct altitude in time—and in his side vision Bucher was aware of the Secretariat building rushing toward them, upon them, and Bucher, concentrating furiously, saw the tall building whip from sight as he yanked the small, improvised lever that loosed him from the Otter's umbilical—hit the equally improvised air rudder with both feet—and the Secretariat building swam back into his line of vision. Only this time he was above it; Bucher's heart leapt for gladness. Dead ahead and perhaps fifty feet below was the south facade of the Secretariat, and between him and the top of the facade stood Kleyr, just as he had seen her before, straight as a reed, face to the night sky, arms held close to her sides.

She did not see Bucher, was not aware of his presence. And, better yet, neither were any of the Al Fat'ha on the roof of the Secretariat. Even Wee-One Rizzick, the giant machete across one shoulder, was engrossed in the ridiculous caperings of Wog Annaser and did not see Bucher's arrival, for the Wog, under the combined influences of hashish and LSD-3, was cavorting insanely about, mouthing Bucher knew not what, nor did he care. All his attention was concentrated

179

on Kleyr; he was not a praying man, but had he been, he might have offered thanks, for he was headed straight toward her on a downward glide path. He shifted both feet from the rudder to the simple mechanism that operated the elevators and would bring the auxiliaries into play, a tiny part of his mind grateful for the ability of David Szold. He was coming in fast! Perhaps too fast! Kleyr stood with eyes closed and—

She grunted explosively when Bucher seized her and pulled her quickly to him, at the same time kicking the elevators with both feet. The sky sail slowed instantly, noticeably; yet they were almost at the opposite end of the diving board before Wee-One Rizzick noticed them. Her deformed mouth flew open to scream as she swept downward powerfully with the machete. The scream and the blow availed her nothing. The scream went unheard, or at least unnoticed, and when she cut the rope Bucher and Kleyr were already tumbling to the roof of the Secretariat building.

"You evil son of a bitch! You kilt Leo, you did! You cut his throat!" Wee-One Rizzick's eyes bulged with maniacal hatred as she screamed these words, but Bucher and Kleyr were busy untangling themselves from the sail and did not notice that the numerous doors opening onto the top floor of the building suddenly burst open, disgorging dozens of the Jewish Defense League, led by none other than Rabbi Shemish.

"You kilt him, you ongrateful son of a bitch!"

Rizzick screamed again, standing over them now, murderous machete raised high in both hands, swinging it at the base of Kleyr's neck as would the beheading executioner. "You kilt Leo—!"

"*Koosh!*"

The ugly Walther in Bucher's big mitt gently loosed its death sigh. The 9mm slug struck Rizzick from the side, at the base of her grotesque hideous nose, the serrated, hollow-point slug blasting most of it from her face, and she dropped the machete instantly, seized her face with both hands, and fled gurgling toward the edge of the roof and disappeared.

"What kept you, lout?" Kleyr asked, blinking back the tears. In his happiness Bucher grinned so hard his face hurt.

"Hairbreadth Harry, that's me. Always just in the nick of time."

"Mmmmm." She nodded, eyeing the sky sail from which he had just freed himself. "I'll have to admit that when you do arrive, you do it in style."

"I ought to bust your rump. Five kidnapped Israelis, when all the while they were at our apartment at the Carlyle—"

She pressed a soft finger against his lips. "Shhhhh. Don't complain. Or haven't you heard? My scheme worked. Egypt signed the non-aggression pact with Israel less than an hour ago. I learned it from the Wog's people. They were talking about it. The Wog is crazy, Boo. Insane. Look."

181

Ali Annaser, who had been wearing his tent-like robe when Bucher arrived, had taken the garment off and now walked about the roof of the Secretariat building naked as a jay bird. He strode about, flapping his arms and crowing like a rooster—and suddenly confronting him was the huge, barrel-chested, bearded Rabbi Shimesh.

"I have always wanted to encounter one of the new Nazis naked," he told the Wog politely. And with this he gave the surprised Wog such a clout at the side of the head the Wog squealed like a castrated pig. And squealed again with the second clout, and also with the third. Oddly, as Bucher looked about the roof, he saw that the Wog's forces had fled into the lower building by way of the doors beside the elevator terminals, all except the tragic Rizzick, leaving none on the roof except him and Kleyr, who was now wrapping herself in the Wog's enormous robe, Rabbi Shimesh, and Ali Annaser, the rabbi repeatedly clubbing the Wog. Gradually, as Bucher watched, Rabbi Shimesh herded Annaser through one of the doors and out of sight.

"Whew!" Bucher said. "It's been a busy day."

"Humph," Kleyr told him impishly. "Just you wait until the morning. Then you can say the same thing about tonight."

THE "BUTCHER,"
the only man to leave
the Mafia—and live!
A man forever on the run,
unable to trust anyone,
condemned to a life
of constant violence!

THE BUTCHER SERIES

THE INCREDIBLE ACTION PACKED SERIES

DEATH MERCHANT

by Joseph Rosenberger

His name is Richard Camellion, he's a master of disguise, deception and destruction. He does what the CIA and FBI cannot do.

Order		Title	Book #	Price
_____	# 1	THE DEATH MERCHANT	P211	$ .95
_____	# 2	OPERATION OVERKILL	P245	$ .95
_____	# 3	THE PSYCHOTRON PLOT	P117	$ .95
_____	# 4	CHINESE CONSPIRACY	P168	$ .95
_____	# 5	SATAN STRIKE	P182	$ .95
_____	# 6	ALBANIAN CONNECTION	P670	$1.25
_____	# 7	CASTRO FILE	P264	$ .95
_____	# 8	BILLIONAIRE MISSION	P339	$ .95
_____	# 9	THE LASER WAR	P399	$ .95
_____	#10	THE MAINLINE PLOT	P473	$1.25
_____	#11	MANHATTAN WIPEOUT	P561	$1.25
_____	#12	THE KGB FRAME	P642	$1.25
_____	#13	THE MATO GROSSO HORROR	P705	$1.25
_____	#14	VENGEANCE OF THE GOLDEN HAWK	P796	$1.25
_____	#15	THE IRON SWASTIKA PLOT	P823	$1.25
_____	#16	INVASION OF THE CLONES	P857	$1.25
_____	#17	THE ZEMLYA EXPEDITION	P880	$1.25

TO ORDER

Please check the space next to the book/s you want, send this order form together with your check or money order, include the price of the book/s and 25¢ for handling and mailing to:
PINNACLE BOOKS, INC. / P.O. BOX 4347
Grand Central Station / New York, N.Y. 10017

☐ CHECK HERE IF YOU WANT A FREE CATALOG

I have enclosed $_____check_____or money order_____
as payment in full. No C.O.D.'s.

Name_____

Address_____

City_____State_____Zip_____
(Please allow time for delivery.)

PB-36